Hope

Right-Side-Up Stories
P.O. Box 1586
Sierra Madre, CA 91025-1586
800-369-9230
626-529-5522
rightsideupstories.com
mjbstory@gmail.com

The story of *The Green Velvet Christmas Dress* has been produced in play form ©2011, 2012

Edited by Marcia Coppess

Illustrations by Janelle Kujath

Amazing Grace, 1779, public domain.

Luke 12:4-9 Scripture quotations from *The Authorized (King James) Version.* Rights in the Authorized Version in the United Kingdom are vested in the Crown. Reproduced by permission of the Crown's patentee, Cambridge University Press.

The New England Primmer ed. 1784, Joseph Addison, "Now I Lay Me Down To Sleep"

Romans 5:6-8 Scripture quotations are taken from the Holy Bible. *New Living Translation* ©1996, 2004, 2015 by Tyndale House Foundation. Used by permission of Tyndale House Publishers, Inc., Carol Stream, Illinois 60188. All rights reserved.

GriefShare is a grief recovery support groups meeting throughout the U.S., Canada, and other countries. griefshare.org

ISBN: 978-0-578-54482-3

The Green Velvet Christmas Dress

A STORY OF HOPE

Written by Melea J. Brock

Illustrations by Janelle Kujath

Dear Living Story,
 reader of *The Green Velvet Christmas Dress*,

I am a part of every story I write. I am a part of this one, too.

I encourage you to read this story aloud to someone, with a group of people, even to yourself. Come on, when was the last time someone told you a story?

This story will take you on a journey of more than century and walk you in and out of history and Christmas! It's my aim that it will speak its hope to an older child, a teen, a young adult, a middle-aged life, a senior adult.

God bless the story you are living out today—may it change someone simply because you live it out loud and on purpose.

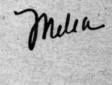

❖ EMMA ❖

T he story begins as all stories begin… with a place, a time and a reason. The green velvet bolt of fabric was as good as sold. Emma had had her eye on its green goodness for almost a year. She would glance at it every time she was in McGeevy's Mercantile and, sometimes, take a moment just to feel its soft rich texture between her fingers. When others eyed its beauty, Mrs. McGeevy would steer them to another more suitable fabric. She had seen Emma look at it longingly when she came into the mercantile.

"May I have it, Father?" she would whisper to God, often.

His answer today was, "Soon, Emma."

How was this soon ever going to happen with a husband working every hour just to make ends meet and her meager sewing work?

So that day, she asked Mrs. McGeevy if she could make a down payment on the bolt of green velvet and pay a little bit of it off each month. To her delight she said, "Yes, consider it your velvet, Emma. I'll have my husband place it on the top shelf."

She wrapped it several times in brown paper and tied it gently with twine. She then wrote "For Emma Harris" on a tag and tied it to the twine. Emma watched as Mr. McGeevy climbed a short step ladder and placed her velvet up on that high shelf where things were set aside for their future owners. The velvet was now next to a long-handled axe and a small wooden crate that read "Hohner Concertina."

She hurried home with all of her things and a small square piece of the green velvet. She was joyous over this decision to put it on hold. There were so many things she could make with the velvet. It was a lovely shade of green, too. Her favorite color had always been green. The color of grass, fields of spring wildflowers with specks of color, wheat and hay before they turn, and, of course, Christmas trees were among her favorite shades of the color green. Her thoughts jumped to the fir tree they had chosen as next year's Christmas tree when they cut last year's down. They had tied two scarlet pieces of ribbon to mark Emily's and William's heights so they could see which had grown more—the children or the tree.

"Luke, I'm going to finish supper up quickly as we have church tonight," she told her faithful horse hitched to the wagon. "And when we all get back home, I'm going to get you a carrot and sketch a few things for my velvet."

She was so thrilled about the velvet. For Emma it already felt like Christmas with the hope of possessing something that she had longed for, as a child does a toy or a doll. She would use every bit of it wisely.

Upon entering her house, her mood of joy immediately changed. Her husband was home, and he was burning something in the fireplace. It was the children's clothes. Confusion overcame Emma. The room was so quiet and still. If her children were home why weren't they filling the room with noise, laughter and a story about some calamity they had with a skunk at school? No, it was too quiet. No joyful hugs or welcoming greetings. Instead, she was met by her husband with a look of concern and a creased brow.

"Emma, the children aren't well."

She felt her stomach drop to the floor. "What's wrong with them?"

"Emily and William both have a fever and are chilled to the bone." His strong voice quavered on the last part of that sentence. She made a start for the bedroom door, but Jackson stopped her.

"Emma, I don't know if you should go in there. I think it's the fever. I'm going to go fetch Doc. They're resting now. I'll be back in an hour."

She collapsed into her husband's arms, feeling lightheaded and overcome by this terrible news. He held her close for a few seconds and then took hold of her shoulders, looked into her worried eyes and said, "Emma, I need you to be strong. I need you to pray and hum lovely songs for your children. Make some dinner for all of us, and something sweet for them. Please, Emma. They need us to be strong. All right?"

She stood up straight and tall, grabbed her apron off the hook near the stove, and stuffed the scrap of green velvet into the pocket of her apron. "Godspeed, Jackson. William and Emily will be fine. We'll all be fine," and she began grabbing pots and pans while humming, "Go Tell It on the Mountain." Jackson hugged her tightly, grabbed his hat, jacket, and a lantern. Then he was gone.

The minute he was out of sight, she cracked the door open and peeked inside her children's room. William and Emily looked fine. A little flushed in the face, but the both of them were sleeping peacefully.

She was nervous and fluttery with all kinds of emotions. Thoughts of childhood illnesses came to mind and with that something she remembered about the fever sweeping through different states and parts of counties far, far away, not anywhere near theirs.

Emma made a hearty vegetable soup, setting aside some of its broth for the children. She also made biscuits and gingerbread. She fed the livestock, milked two cows, fed the dogs, and still no husband or Doc.

Throwing caution and the warning to the wind, she had checked the children at least a dozen times and applied cold compresses to their foreheads. They didn't stir except when she replaced the compresses. She sang every carol and hymn to them that she knew. And then, finally, she heard the rustle of approaching horses and a wagon. There was a quick exchange shared with Doc, and Jackson led him to the children's room.

Finally, Jackson emerged.

"What did he say?"

"Nothing yet. He's still examining them. Is that gingerbread I smell?" And he sniffed the air like William did when he smelled something sweet. Emma ladled some soup into a bowl and grabbed a few biscuits.

"Jack, you need to eat." Jackson took his wife's hands in his. "You need to eat, too. We both will need our strength for whatever is ahead."

Emma began to pray, "Father, we need you. Please spare our children. Your Word says in Psalm 91 that sickness and disease will not come near the house of your beloved ones. Please Father," her voice broke, and her tears began to splash on the table.

Jackson finished the prayer, and as he let go of Emma's hands, she realized his hand felt a little clammy. She tried to brush the thought aside and they began to eat.

Finally, Doc emerged from the bedroom. He crossed slowly over to the table and sat down. Emma jumped up to get him a bowl of soup. "No, Emma. Coffee will do me just fine. I need you to sit down here with Jackson."

She placed her hands in her apron pocket to pull out her hankie and her fingers brushed against the softness of the velvet.

"Well, your children are just beautiful. I can't believe how William has shot up. He's nearly as tall as Emily now."

"They both said they'd like some gingerbread, and I told them just a little piece in case their stomach didn't take kindly to it. Such sweet children." Then Doc's face became very serious. "I believe we are dealing with the fever, and with both of them."

Jackson took in a deep breath as hot tears began to flow down Emma's cheeks. She quickly wiped them away. He then took hold of one of Emma's hand. Doc went on to explain that they would need to stay quarantined as a family. "The whole farm really," added Doc.

He said he would be speaking with Reverend Michaels very soon about a way to get food and supplies to them daily, starting the next morning.

"In fact, Reverend Michaels will be picking me up shortly. I asked him to do this, as I want you here with your family, Jackson."

All three of them had been exposed to the fever in the past, so they would likely be fine. Doc did add that it was very important for both of them to keep up their strength, so that they could take care of the children. Instructions were written out; medicine handed over, and a time was set for Doc's next visit.

"You can expect me about sun-up."

"We'll have something warm for you to eat," said Emma.

"Both of you need to rest whenever you can. May God's will be done on earth as it is in Heaven in this home tonight." It was a blessing and a benediction.

They both watched as Revered Michaels and Doc drove away. And with their departure a feeling of darkness, stronger than the night's, came into their house. Instinctively, Emma and Jackson walked into their children's room, knelt down, and began to pray over them. After several moments of quiet prayer that could've moved mountains, Emma and Jackson began to sing over their children—something that they did every night.

Fresh morning sunlight poured through the bedroom window as a knock on the door startled Emma and Jackson. The night had been a long one with each parent taking shifts replacing compresses and getting the children to take sips of water. There were the doses of medicine (which they didn't like in the least), the changing of drenched bed clothes, fanning of their warm bodies, the reading of stories, and the singing of favorite songs and hymns.

Each of them was lying across a child's bed and immediately noticed the children's breathing seemed more labored than it did hours earlier. Jackson hurried to the door and let Doc inside.

"How are they?" he asked Jackson.

"Their breathing is different… like it's an effort now."

Doc was a man of few words, but they were always honest and comforting ones. He was a minister for a short time before entering medical school. People often referenced Jesus' disciple, Luke the great physician, in describing his manner. However, his heart was on his sleeve this morning.

"You and Emma go and check on your livestock and get some fresh air while I examine your children."

Then Doc noticed the sweat around Jackson's shirt collar and chest. "Are you all right, Jackson?"

"I'm fine. Tired though. It was a sleepless night for both of us."

Emma immediately began stoking the stove fire and placed the large metal kettle on for coffee and tea. Her only solace was her constant busyness. She grabbed both of their coats and gloves, and they headed out to the barn.

Cows mooed, chickens scratched and picked at the dirt hungry for their seed, and the horses whinnied for their hay unaware of what was happening in the house. Everything seemed right in the barn. Emma let her mind drift on the thought of how it must have been the night Christ was born, surrounded by some of the same creatures that filled up this space. The two of them were so busy with the usual morning chores that they hadn't noticed Doc had stepped into the barn.

"Jackson and Emma—can we talk?"

Doc kicked at the dirt on the floor of the barn as they hurried to his side.

"Emily and William are not better. The fever has increased in both of them. Their hearts are strong, but their lungs are filling up with fluid. Are they coughing at all?"

"No," they both said.

"Yes, I observed this as well. It was quite a struggle to get them to take a deep breath and cough voluntarily. I gave them some expectorant, and they seemed to tolerate it. We'll need to see if the expectorant brings any of the fluid up and out of those lungs."

Doc stopped for a second, measuring his next words carefully. Jackson and Emma held one another's gloved hands even tighter.

"However, if we don't see any improvement by midday, we will need to prepare for…"

"Please Doc, don't say it," Emma said cutting his sentence short. "We will prepare, Doc. We will prepare for Christmas. Jackson, get the Christmas tree that we tied the scarlet ribbons on last year. And while you're up there doing that, I will start working on our Christmas dinner. The ham is cured by now, and I have all those jars of spiced peaches and green beans, and plenty of potatoes. We'll give the children their presents early. They'll be so happy to get them early, and it will do them a world of good, too. I just know it. I just know it will."

Jackson and Doc had been watching Emma as she swirled around the barn describing the future preparations for Christmas. It was distracting from the heavy truth of the moment and sounded quite wonderful.

"Doc, will you stay for Christmas supper?" There was a desperate plea in the eyes of that young mother and father. The good doctor wasn't going anywhere. This family needed hope and they needed to not be alone for what was ahead.

"How could I not?" He turned to a worried father, "Jackson, do you need any help with that Christmas tree of yours?"

"I sure do, Doc." Jackson was grateful for this offer of help and a brief escape to the hills from the painful story unfolding in his family. By the time the rig was hitched to the wagon, Doc had checked the children one more time, and instructions had been given to Emma about the right dose of the new medicine.

God's everlasting mercies are no small thing. The children had their last Christmas with all of the magic that Christmas brings with it. That evening they passed in the arms of their mother and father.

"It was an amazing moment that I will never forget," Doc recalled to others later on. "We sat in the darkness of the children's room, with Emma and Jackson holding both of them. The room was lit by only a solitary kerosene lamp, but their room...." His voice always broke up as he told it: "Their bedroom was filled with a light and a mist that I've never seen here on this earth. The unmistakable presence of God was in the room! We couldn't speak as we watched those children, who hadn't moved for hours, open their eyes. And with an indescribable joy creasing their faces, they lifted their hands to Someone." Doc would always add with a certainty and through tears, "And that Someone was our good Lord, Jesus."

That was a gift from God for Emma and Jackson; and for Doc too. "We didn't speak as the presence of God lingered in the room to comfort all of us. And then He was gone. After it was over, Death came in with all of its loud silence."

A deep pain-filled weeping poured out of poor Jackson and Emma. There was no comfort on this earth that could have consoled these two parents. Doc cried right along with them. After a bit, he took a small Bible out of his doctor's bag, opened it to Psalm 23, and began to read God's words over both of them. He then went to other passages of scripture in Psalm 34, Psalm 139, Lamentations 3, John 14, Romans 8, and ended with Matthew 5:4: *"Blessed are those who mourn for they shall be comforted."*

He then prayed for God's everlasting comfort to be upon Emma and Jackson in a way that they'd never known before in all of their lives. He encouraged them to let people help them, and to not be afraid to accept it no matter how small or large it seemed. "You can't do this alone, Emma and Jackson. Let us help you."

Doc also advised them to bury the children on their farm, but away from the livestock and the fields. Some men who had been exposed to the fever when they were young rode out to the farm that afternoon and helped a weakened Jackson and Emma do the hardest thing a parent ever has to do— bury their children. They helped them take William's and Emily's bodies to the spreading oak tree that they loved to climb on and play under. Reverend Michaels came and tried his best to console and care for this now childless couple. Two simple white crosses marked the children's final resting places.

People in town began to send them food immediately, along with flowers, letters, and hand-made cards by the children from the school. They were a much-beloved family. For death to have touched them in such a quick and tragic way seemed unreal and unfair to all who knew them.

Jackson and Emma's sobering words were read by Reverend Michaels at a town meeting that was called several days after the children's passing:

> *The Lord gives, and the Lord takes away.*
> *Blessed be the name of the Lord, forever.*
> *His Hope does not disappoint us.*
> *Hold onto this Hope with us.*
> *Thank you for your care, your food, gifts, and kindnesses*
> *that have nourished us and reminded us that we are not alone.*
> *— Jackson & Emma Harris*

 **2**

Jackson finally collapsed from exhaustion into a deep sleep that lasted 24 hours. He woke up weak and very sad. Emma sensed it might be the fever, but her heart hoped it was just the complications of grief and fatigue. She asked a neighbor to fetch Doc for her. He confirmed what she already knew.

"Emma, I am so sorry. Make your husband comfortable and say everything you need to say to one another now."

Jackson was a strong man. He lived three more days.

How Emma was able to do the things she did astounded her as well as all of those around her. Emma made another Christmas dinner. This time, it was turkey with all the trimmings. Jackson was able to sit up for some of it, eating very little.

They spent the hours that remained in each other's arms talking, laughing, and recalling the goodness of their 10 years of marriage. They talked about the wonder, the beauty, and the gift of Emily and William. Emma wrote her Christmas poem and read it to Jackson. He told her where her Christmas gift was hidden. It was a new sewing basket. She talked of the green velvet that she had put on hold at the McGeevy's Mercantile and shared some of her beginning sketches of the things she hoped to make someday.

"Emma, I want you to make that dress right there." Jackson pointed with great effort to a place on the page. She squeezed his hand and whispered, "I will, my love."

They sang Christmas hymns to one another and then Emma sang *"Amazing Grace"* over Jackson, savoring every verse, especially the words: *"Yea, when this flesh and heart shall fail, and mortal life shall cease, I shall possess within the veil, a life of joy and peace."* Emma woke up the next morning with Jackson's hand resting on hers. He had passed during the night. A beautiful smile creased his face, reminiscent of the children's faces.

Death knocked on the door of her home and walked in like it owned the place. It stoked the fires of loneliness. It set her table and filled it up with confusion, resentment and anger. It whispered lies to her: "Emma, you're all alone now. Even God has left you now. See what happens when you pray? People die."

Doc, Reverend Michaels, and several neighbors came to help her bury Jackson's body right next to the children. Someone began to care for her livestock, and others helped with the fields and orchards. Women came and cleaned every inch of her home and anything that the fever had touched. The mattresses, linens, blankets, and quilts were burned and replaced by new ones.

Neighbors filled her cupboards and made food for her. They sat with Emma, day and night, as she rocked back and forth in silence, holding the photograph of her family. Every now and then she would whisper the same words, "Your kindness will be rewarded by the Lord," but that's all she could say as tears flowed for days and days.

But one by one, everyone returned to their homes and their lives, leaving her all alone. Death came and whispered those same ugly words, once again, adding a new phrase: "Sorrow lives here now." And Emma believed it.

3

After several months of darkness and sadness, Emma woke up and realized she had slept through a whole night, and in her bed instead of the rocker. She got dressed, fed her own livestock, put on her apron, and began to make something to eat. She felt hungry. Hunger was something she hadn't felt for a while. In fact, she wanted biscuits, so she made dozens of them. She finally sat down to eat one. It was still warm from the oven and spread with a thick layer of strawberry preserves. It was like tasting spring and summer, all at the same time.

Her mind drifted back to the strawberries she and the children had planted that comprised that jar of jam. Her eyes began to moisten with tears. Instinctively, she reached into her apron pocket for a hankie, and her fingertips brushed over something soft and plush and with the prick of a straight pin. She pulled out the familiar scrap of fabric and found a small note attached to it:

Dear Emma, Come pick up your green velvet when it's time.
It's yours now. Sorry for this deep and lasting loss you have suffered.
Love, Mr. & Mrs. McGeevy

She let her thoughts about the treasured bolt of green velvet fill up her mind. She even thought about putting on a freshly pressed dress, hitching up one of the horses, and riding into town to pick it up. But the task seemed so enormous. Impossible. So she ate another biscuit.

She was taking out the last tray of biscuits when she heard a knock at the door. It was Mr. and Mrs. McGeevy and Reverend Michaels. She hadn't even heard them approach, nor the barking of her dogs. She recalled that Jackson told her that when someone takes the time to come to your door you should open it because it just might be the Lord or an angel. She was quite the sight, but she smoothed her hair back, took a deep breath, and opened the door.

The minute they saw her, their eyes filled with tears and they said familiar words of consolation she'd been hearing for months now. But before they could say another word Emma said, "Please, come in. I have biscuits that are hot, and the water for tea is ready."

The three of them were taken aback by this unexpected and generous greeting. They came inside and sat down at Emma's table that she quickly covered with a tablecloth and set with the help of Mrs. McGeevy.

"Reverend Michaels, I know that you like your tea with milk and sugar. Mr. and Mrs. McGeevy, how do you take yours?"

Still amazed by Emma, they mumbled something to her about their preferences. Within moments warm biscuits, butter, jam, spiced peaches, and fresh cream were spread before them.

Reverend Michaels offered thanks for biscuits and peaches at 11 o'clock in the morning, the gift of life and breath, for Emma's kindness to them, and other words that might have brought comfort to someone else. Not so for Emma. She was having a hard time with this thing called prayer. She had prayed and prayed that God would spare her children's and her husband's lives. She didn't understand prayer anymore. She had told God, "I will speak with You when my sorrow is no more."

Now, the Lord God Almighty doesn't take orders from us. His love reaches to us and woos us to Him. And Emma was about to receive some of His amazing love and His grace. Emma stared at the four place settings while the Reverend went on and on, or so it seemed to her ears. She hadn't used her china and these four place settings since they all had passed. She stared at the blue willow pattern remembering the day the china had arrived in a big wooden barrel at the mercantile.

The amen must have been said because the three of them began to compliment her on her delicious biscuits and spiced peaches. And about how nice she looked, and how well her livestock seemed. A fight rose up in Emma. Her question was going to put an end to all of the seemingly trivial conversation being passed back and forth.

"Are we the only family?"

They all knew what she meant. A bit of silence passed before Reverend Michaels spoke. "Yes. We believe the immediate care that Doc, Jackson, and you took as the fever hit your household spared our whole town. Emma, everyone is deeply grateful to you and Jackson."

She stood up and refreshed the hot water in the teapot. She wanted to scream something ugly and mean. Then she heard a still small voice say, "Emma, listen and receive."

Mrs. McGeevy excused herself and went out to the wagon, picked up a large basket, and quickly stepped back inside. It was filled with the bolt of familiar fabric and tons of sewing notions. "We have some things for you, Emma! Your pretty green velvet, a piece of lining that we can purchase more of, some needles, spools of thread, a pair of the best scissors I've ever used. Honestly, they cut like butter. There are also two pin cushions and a silver thimble engraved with your initials."

Emma received the basket with gracious arms. She then hugged Mrs. McGeevy and thanked her for the green velvet and everything else that she'd been given. Mrs. McGeevy asked what she planned to do with the velvet.

"I don't know really, and I don't know if I will remember how to sew. I haven't made anything for a very long time."

"Of course, you will remember." Mrs. McGeevy took Emma's slender hands in hers. "These hands will remember. And it will be beautiful."

Mr. McGeevy let that thoughtful word from his wife hang in the air for a little bit, before he spoke. "Now, Emma the next thing we've brought to you is from the whole town. Would you walk out to our wagon with us?"

Mrs. McGeevy grabbed Emma's shawl off a hook near the door and wrapped it around her shoulders. It was a bright day, and the sunlight stung Emma's eyes. Reverend Michaels took her by the arm as they walked to the back of the wagon. They didn't say a thing. Instead they let Emma read the stone marker and take it all in. "We'd like to go up to where your family is buried and place it there today, if that's all right with you."

Emma began to cry. "I wanted one just like this. How did you all know?"

They told her that the stone cutter, Mr. Giles, felt directed by God in the design for the family stone. He reported it was as if the good Lord put His hands on him as he made it. This touched Emma, as Jasper Giles and Jackson had been good friends.

"We can do it another day, Emma," said Reverend Michaels, sensing that she was overwhelmed by these gestures.

"No, I will receive these gifts and be grateful for the kindnesses shown to my family and me this day." She said all of that through the tears one cries as they realize they are deeply loved at a newer level than they understood before. Emma took a deep breath. She knew Reverend Michaels, Doc, and the McGeevy's loved her but today's outpouring of love represented an unearthly kind of love. Her own nature for weeks on end had been about protecting her feelings, her thoughts, and staying inside her home where no one could see her sorrow and undone grief.

Mr. McGeevy headed to the barn for shovels while Mrs. McGeevy took Emma's arm again. "Let's go get your bonnet, Emma. It's a sunny day. Then we can go find something from your garden to lay at the, the—"

Emma kindly saved her from saying the word '*graves*.' "Yes, flowers would be nice but not much is blooming right now. I do have some hawthorn sprigs in water, and we can cut some fresh pine branches to add to them. I could tie them all up with a strip of some of the green velvet."

What happened next was truly amazing. Word had already been passed throughout their small town when the gravestone was loaded into the wagon that morning. The news, with Mr. and Mrs. McGeevy's absence at the mercantile, alerted the town that it was a "go" on all they had planned days earlier. People slipped from their fields, the schoolhouse, their washing, cleaning, cooking, and many other things. All of them took the time to walk or ride out beyond the fields of Emma and Jackson's farm, to the spreading oak where the three white crosses had been placed.

Many of them were already there when Emma and the others arrived at the tree. There stood Doc with his wife, Elizabeth, along with many people Emma hadn't seen since it had all started. There were those that had helped bury her family, and those who helped her put her home back together after it was all over. Those that had tended to her fields and to her livestock. There were several dozen children running about under the oak, many of whom were schoolmates of William and Emily, along with their teacher, Mrs. Blackwood. Everyone had come to pay their respects and to show Emma their gratitude for all she had done to save their town, their very lives.

It took half a dozen men to lift the heavy stone marker from the wagon with Mr. Giles supervising. In moments, a portion of the earth had been dug out and leveled for its placement. Once the gravestone was set, men, women, and children placed flowers at its base, then stepped back to form a large circle. Emma stepped away from the circle to bend down and place her bouquet at their grave. Tears splashed on the hawthorn, pine sprigs, and green velvet. Reverend Michaels and his wife placed their hands on Emma's shoulders as she quietly sobbed.

Finally, her tears subsided and Emma looked at the marker. Really looked at it. The words carved deep into the stone were the blessing her husband had spoken many times at the end of a prayer. She let her fingers trace their names—Jackson, William, and Emily. Mr. Giles had etched a large pine tree and two little pine trees into the stone. Their names and the dates of their births and deaths were under each pine tree. It was stunning and simple.

Emma stood up and leaned against the cold gravestone. She shared how much she missed the everyday things of their presence here on earth—their faces, their voices, the sound of their steps, their laughter, their stories and humorous ways, their likes and dislikes, their expressions of joy, sadness, surprise, pain, anger, gentleness, strength, and comfort. She spoke words of thanks and gratitude over the watchful care of her life and the farm, and of her indebtedness for such a meaningful tribute to her family. Her eloquence and kind words were touching and brought many to tears as they thought of their own finite lives. Reverend Michaels ended the graveside gathering with a prayer and the same words etched upon their gravestone.

The Lord watch between me and thee
while we are absent one from another.

The McGeevys drove Emma to the schoolhouse where a late supper had been prepared by some of the women. There was something final and celebratory about it. People shared stories about Jackson, Emily, and William, along with words of encouragement for Emma. She found herself laughing several times, and oh how good it felt to laugh and to remember them with others. She felt hope again. It was small bit of hope, but it didn't feel temporary this time. In fact, it felt like something had been planted in her heart from the tiniest of seeds. She sensed it could grow, with time.

That night Emma slept in the deepest peace she'd known since their passing.

The days that followed the graveside and memorial swung between fits of sadness and a very real hope that Emma could no longer deny. The sadness was different now. Emma had learned to shoo the negativity of death away and out of her house, like one would do with an mangy stray cat looking for scraps. A simple prayer of "Be gone, in Jesus's name," and it would leave.

She would head up to the spreading oak and spend her day talking to the three of them, especially when she felt overcome by their absence. The gravestone did more than mark the value of her family. It marked a story in the earth that time could not erase. "I will never forget you," she would say as she touched the stone and headed back to her home each time.

Once a week, Emma hitched up her horses to the wagon and went into town. She'd always purchase a few things to eat from the mercantile. Her shopping list remained meager—fresh fruits and vegetables, flour, sugar, beans, rice, and licorice to remind her of the children. Mrs. Mc-Geevy would always place a few extras in the baskets that Emma brought with her.

Someone came and plowed and seeded the fields and tended to the apple orchards. The chickens seemed well fed, the cows were milked daily, and a small bucket of fresh milk draped with an embroidered tea towel (to keep the flies away) was brought to Emma's door each morning. She had quite a collection of these embroidered tea towels now. She kept washing them in hopes of returning them with a thank you to someone. The wood piled up outside her front door. Even her dogs enjoyed a bone or two from some friendly person. Whomever they were, the dogs liked them as they never barked. She had a feeling it was her neighbors to the north of her farm. When Reverend Michaels dropped by and asked how she was doing she'd say to him, "Finding my way, Reverend. Finding my way down the dark hall of their absence from this earth."

Mrs. McGeevy would also drop by to check in on Emma. Every now and then she would ask, "Have you started on your green velvet?"

"Not yet, Mrs. McGeevy. It's not time yet."

She was a round, happy, determined little woman, and she did her best to bring Emma a little further out of the sadness with each visit. "I think there's some goodness in that green velvet of yours, Emma. I truly do believe there is," she'd say. "I cannot wait to see what your hands will create."

"Oh, Mrs. McGeevy, you always believe the best in me."

"I do and I mean every word of it, Emma. You've won blue ribbons at the county fair with those hands. Whatever you create, it will be beautiful."

"Mrs. McGeevy, you have me blushing now," said Emma, fanning herself with a tea towel.

Mrs. McGeevy took Emma's hands into hers as she had done when she brought the green velvet to her. With tears she said, "Emma, these hands have touched a little bit of heaven and when they touch that green velvet, something amazing and eternal is going to come forth." Tears rolled down each woman's cheeks with those words. Emma became very quiet with this thought. It sounded big and kind of prophetic. She looked up to the top shelf of her cupboard where the bundled velvet had been placed many weeks ago.

"Surely you've thought of that, too, Emma." Mrs. McGeevy also looked up to the cupboard. "It's up there … just waiting for you."

Emma felt something stirring in her with these words of Mrs. McGeevy. "Someday soon, you'll take it down from that high shelf, unroll its beauty, and begin to sew that bit of eternity into the goodness in the green velvet."

4

It was a pleasant early day in spring. Emma woke up feeling hopeful. The sun poured through the windows in her bedroom. She still felt something stirring in her from that moment the day before with Mrs. McGeevy. As she sipped her morning coffee, she thought about her last words to her "… there's a goodness in the green velvet."

She dressed quickly, grabbed the leather-bound journal Jackson had made, a couple of pencils from her daughter's school treasure box, and packed some things to eat, along with a canteen of water.

Today, the grave of her family didn't feel as lonely as it had on other days. She spread a quilt on the grassy ground next to them and began sketching more details on a previous drawing of a dress. It was the one she had shown to Jackson the night he passed. That thought brought a flash of sadness. She wanted to rip the drawing out of her journal, crumple it up and throw it away. But another thought, like a still small voice, rose up from somewhere deep in her heart and told her to save it.

Hours later, she had sketched a new version of that dress. It was a modest and elegant one that could be worn to a wedding, a night of theater, or a dinner reception at a fancy hotel in Chicago. Her mind wandered to how this sort of a dress could have been used for her daughter's trousseau or something she would have worn to her own children's weddings. A lonely darkness rose up in her like storm clouds with that last thought. Again, a voice in her heart saved her, *It's beautiful, Emma.* This time she fought her tears instead of giving in to them.

At that very moment several little birds hopped along the ground nearby, right where she was sitting. They were so close she could have touched them. Instead she stayed completely still. They were rooting in the grass for food. They hopped over to the crust of bread that remained from her meal and eagerly began to eat.

She giggled to herself. *Two... now there's three birds, Lord?* And soon there were more of them. Five, six, seven little sparrows, nibbling away on the treasure she had discarded. Emma remembered the passage out of the Gospels.

> *Don't be afraid. For you are more valuable to*
> *God than a whole flock of sparrows.*

And the sadness stopped. As fast as it had come, it stopped. She quietly grabbed a pencil, some paper and began sketching the little gathering eating their meal. She wanted a picture of this moment of bliss. She sketched several little sparrows picking at a crust of bread, with several others waiting patiently in the background for their turn. After that, she packed up her things and sat on the edge of the great tombstone that marked their three lives. "Look at this, all of you. What do you think? I am going to make this dress and I'm going to start on it today." She gathered up her things and walked back to her home, singing all the way.

It was moving toward three in the afternoon as Emma had spent the better part of the day near their grave. She stoked the stove and moved the pot of soup from the day before onto it. She grabbed an apple and began munching on it. She knew she would need the sustenance for the task ahead. She lit all of her lamps and stoked the fire ebbing in her fireplace. She then cleared off the table and wiped it clean.

Finally, she took down the bolt of green velvet that had sat way up there for months. She unwrapped it, preserving the brown paper, twine and the tag. She then unrolled it and sized up the beauty and softness between her fingertips. She held an edge of it close to her cheek and remembered how soft velvet truly felt upon a cheek.

Taking her sketch from earlier that day, Emma began chalking the dress's bodice and sleeves onto the brown paper that the velvet had been wrapped in. She cut them out, pinned them together, and then pinned the sample to her body. Checking them in her full-length mirror, she thought, "Hmmm, maybe a little smaller here, and a little larger there." She had lost some weight over the last several months but didn't want to make the pattern too small. After all, someone else might be stepping into its green goodness someday.

She had already decided that she was going to do something different with the sleeves. Not puffy and large, as was the fashion, but gathered closer on one's arm. Perhaps she'd set a new fashion for women, she mused. Emma had never been one to follow the fashion of the day. Practical. Simple. Modest. That was her style.

The velvet material was already so extravagant compared to her usual cotton garments. She'd keep the drape in the skirt, letting the fabric carry the beauty and the detail of one flounce at the bottom of the dress. A few simple touches like a wide waistband, stand-up collar, the rounded but closer sleeves, and some well-placed covered buttons would finish the design.

She gathered up all of her sewing supplies and the wonderful scissors that Mrs. McGeevy had said were the best set of shears she'd ever used. She pinned the bodice and the sleeve patterns to the velvet and chalked out the outline of each piece. Then Emma then said a little prayer. Any seamstress will say that the first cut into a length of fabric, especially a silk or a velvet, is a take-a-deep-breath-moment.

"Father, if there truly is a goodness in the green velvet, then bring it forth as I cut out this dress and begin to make it. Thank you for my steady hands. Amen."

It was true. The scissors did cut the velvet like butter. "Thank you, Mrs. McGeevy!" she said out loud. In her heart she could hear a cheery reply echo back to her.

By evening's end, Emma had the dress's bodice and sleeves basted together, and the sleeves attached with pins to the bodice. Her eyes were beginning to feel the strain of working in the lamp light and her back was stiff from standing over the table, measuring, re-measuring, chalking, pinning, and cutting. She decided to leave everything where it was. She certainly wasn't expecting any guests the next day.

She took out the little sketch of the sparrows from earlier that day. She placed it on top of the mantle and sat down in front of the fireplace with a cup of chamomile tea. She stared at it, pondering it and the meaning of the scripture on sparrows and their value to the Lord. Taking the family Bible from its place on the mantle, she turned to the Gospel of Luke, chapter 12 and read aloud, starting at verse 4.

⁴And I say unto you my friends, be not afraid of them that kill the body, and after that have no more that they can do. ⁵But I will forewarn you whom ye shall fear: Fear him, which after he hath killed hath power to cast into hell; yea, I say unto you, Fear him. ⁶Are not five sparrows sold for two farthings, and not one of them is forgotten before God? [7]But even the very hairs of your head are all numbered. Fear not therefore: ye are of more value than many sparrows. [8]Also I say unto you, Whosoever shall confess me before men, he shall the Son of man also confess before the angels of God: [9]But he that denieth me before men shall be denied before the angels of God.

Emma flipped the Bible open to the first few pages, where she knew her family's names were written down. She looked at their names and this time, she smiled. *I am more valuable than sparrows. I am not forgotten. Who are we to think of ourselves as anything less than valuable to you, Father?*

She let her mind drift back to the dark times of feeling so lost, alone, and forgotten by God and man. Then her mind was quickened to this morning. It had been such a good day. For the first time in a very long time she felt God's hand resting on her shoulder. That was something she hadn't felt in a long time—not since before Jackson's passing. She instinctively reached over and touched her right shoulder thinking, *I feel your joy over me this day, Father. Thank you.*

There it was, again. Prayer. Emma was talking to God—something she hadn't done for a long time. It felt like it was a conversation, too. She looked at her hands on her lap. *Such busy hands today, Father.*

She placed the Bible back on the mantle and blew out all of the lamplights save the one she'd carry to her bedroom. She dressed for bed and brushed her hair remembering that every one of her hairs were counted by the Lord. She tucked herself down deep into her covers. She was feeling a great sense of peace, accomplishment, and excitement for the next day. As she drifted off to sleep, she recited the prayer she'd taught her children:

Now I lay me down to sleep, I pray the Lord, my soul to keep; Guide and guard me through the night. And wake me with the morning's light. Amen.

Emma awoke the next day with the morning light feeling even more alive than the previous day. She drank her coffee and ate two biscuits spread with butter and strawberry preserves. The preserves were from a year ago, and they still tasted just like summer. If summer has a taste it is a handful of freshly picked ripe strawberries, rinsed with cold water, she thought to herself.

Peter, the neighbor on the farm to the north, had just placed milk at her front door. It was a daily chore, among many, that he had been doing for months now. She had figured out where the embroidered tea towels had come from, too. They were from Peter's wife, Margaret.

She opened the door and called after him. "Peter, thank you! I appreciate the fresh milk that you bring me each morning. What can I do to repay you for all of these kindnesses—the tending to my animals, the wood you've chopped, the field work, even the bones for Bartholomew and Jacob?"

Peter must have looked quite surprised that Emma was even talking to him. In all these weeks and months since taking over the Harris farm's chores he had barely seen Emma, let alone spoken with her. He knew her question was a serious one. Peter took off his hat and nervously twisted it in his hands.

"I'm glad I could be here for you, Ma'am. Could you say a prayer for my Pa? He's not feeling well today." Peter took a deep breath and then asked, "And when the time is right, could Margaret come over for a visit? And, if it's not too much trouble, could you teach her how to make biscuits like yours? Yours float in the air. Hers fall to the ground. And please, you didn't hear that from me."

Emma quietly laughed at his biscuit description. She had left warm biscuits for Peter on days when she couldn't show her face. She set them out on the bench where he left the milk. She'd wrap them in one of Margaret's embroidered tea towels, along with some apple butter or a piece of ham and cheese. He usually sat down on her bench and ate them right there. She knew this recipe request was a genuine one. Apparently, a very serious one, too.

"Peter, I will pray for your Pa. And yes, I would love the company of Margaret. Please tell her that I could use her help with some canning this week. Any day is fine for me."

Peter's face widened into a huge grin. "I will be forever grateful to you for this, Emma. Margaret asks about you every day." Peter pulled his hat back on, jumped on his horse and rode away.

Hmmm, Emma thought. *Biscuits that float in the air. No one has ever described them like that before. I'm highly complimented, Peter.*

5

Margaret came the next afternoon with canning jars and some of her supplies. She was ready to help Emma can vegetables or fruit. Emma asked Margaret if she would mind helping her make some stew and biscuits first. She hadn't felt much like eating, but could eat that for days.

Margaret seemed a little nervous, but very happy. She and Peter had been married several years and still, no children. Her embroidered towels had been like sweet little messages to Emma—an apple, a strawberry, a tiny bouquet of flowers, a bird, the sun… even one with Bartholomew and Jacob with a bone.

"Sure, Emma. I love the smell of a pot of stew on the back burner—most days." Margaret then took a hankie out of her sleeve and began fanning herself and talking very quickly. "I haven't told many people this news, Emma. You're one of the first to know. I'm, I'm…" Suddenly Margaret's happy face turned pale, almost green. She ran to the sink and gave up a good portion of her last meal. Taking a breath and coming up from the sink they both said the word together: "Pregnant!" Then they both began to laugh.

"I'm so sorry, Emma. What a way to get to know your neighbor!"

Emma helped Margaret to the rocking chair. She ran water over two cloths, wrung them out, and handed them to her. "There, there. Place one of these on your forehead. I'm going to make you some ginger tea."

"Ginger tea? No, thank you. I don't think I could stomach it." Emma assured Margaret that this was one of the best remedies for morning sickness, and that she would feel much better after she had a cup of it. Emma hummed as she placed the water on the stove and gathered two china teacups and saucers from the cupboard. "Emma, does this ever go away?"

She smiled remembering the very same feeling when her morning sickness lingered on and on with Emily. "Give it a few more weeks."

The two of them sat and chatted about the medicinal uses of ginger. Margaret's color returned to her cheeks and she began to feel much better. She said Peter would love a boy, she a girl but that they would both be happy no matter what the good Lord gave to them. She asked Emma if she remembered that she had been pregnant two years ago, and shared about miscarrying their child at 12 weeks.

"I wasn't sick like this at all. I felt great. And then it happened. Doc came after it was over. He was very kind, patted my hand, and assured me that I'd be all right. But I wasn't all right. In those few weeks that I was with child, I had planned out his entire life. I felt like I wept forever. No one seemed to understand or care about my pain. I waited for someone to say, 'I am so sorry for your loss, Margaret.'

"Do you remember the Sunday that you said those words to me? You took my hands in yours and placed a jar of strawberry jam in them."

Tears filled her eyes as Margaret went on with her story. "You said to me, 'Someday, it will feel like summer again. And when it does open up this jar and taste and see that the Lord is good to you, Margaret'."

This confession was too much for Emma. Her own words of compassion over the loss of a loved one spoken back to her by this young mother touched a place deep inside of her. There was no need for more words. They silently shared the strong kinship of loss, that quiet understanding and peace one feels when they've been heard and valued for their story.

Margaret stood up and said, "I feel so much better now, Emma. That tea of yours is amazing! Thank you for listening to me. Let's get to making that stew for your dinner tonight."

Emma said, "All right. Let's start with the biscuits first." She added with a smile, "I have a jar of strawberry jam that I opened this morning."

Margaret stoked the stove fire, and Emma gathered the ingredients for biscuits. Emma asked Margaret if she had ever tried buttermilk in her biscuits. Margaret said that she had always followed her mama's recipe. They discovered that each of them had lost their mother at a young age. In less than an hour they were eating warm biscuits spread with strawberry jam. Margaret thought they were the best biscuits that she had ever tasted! She was amazed that she didn't feel nauseous after eating one. She asked if she could take a half a dozen or more home with her for Peter and Pa.

"Absolutely—and some ginger root powder for your tea," added Emma.

Margaret admitted that Peter didn't care for her biscuits. "I find them on the side of plates with one bite gone, wrapped up in a napkin, or in the dog's dish. Our dog doesn't like them either." This made Emma smile to herself as she remembered Peter's expressive comments about her biscuits.

Emma wrapped several of them up in a tea towel and placed them in a basket covered in one of Margaret's tea towels. She said how much the embroidered tea towels had brightened her heart on many a dark day.

In another hour there was a hearty stew on the back burner filling Emma's house with its delicious smell. The women chattered away about everything—from hearty soups to spiced walnuts. Emma showed Margaret the green velvet dress sketch and the bodice with its sleeves pinned into place. She gently slipped it over Margaret's arms, pinned it together in the back and then led her to the dressing mirror. "Will you look at that! It fits you, too, Margaret."

"Not for long!" And they both laughed. "It's so pretty and soft, Emma. And I love the color you chose: green!" Her eyes filled with tears. "I will never forget this day with you."

Emma agreed with her and asked Margaret about her baby's anticipated arrival. "December! It's such a perfect time for a child to be born, isn't it?" Emma's heart sank a little at this thought but then it rose up again knowing there would be a new little life in this world.

Margaret asked Emma when she'd return to church. Emma replied that she had thought about returning to church, but it felt too hard. The thought of sitting with Margaret, Peter, and his father felt a little less lonely. She hugged Margaret and handed her the basket of biscuits and some ginger tea that she had prepared. She whispered, "I will sit with all of you when I do come back to church."

Margaret hugged Emma tightly. It meant so much to this young expectant mother to know there was someone just down the road that she could lean on. It was just as wonderful for Emma to know there was a young family just up the road that cared so deeply for her. She had done nothing to deserve their kindness.

"You have brought an unmistakable joy into my home, Margaret. Please, come back anytime."

"Next week we will can something. I can't wait to see more of the green velvet Christmas dress when I return."

This description tickled Emma and she repeated the words with emphasis and a question mark: "The green velvet Christmas dress?"

"Yes, the green velvet Christmas dress. That's what you're making, and maybe that's when you'll wear it for the first time—at Christmas, Emma."

"Maybe," echoed Emma. It didn't feel like a dare to her ears. It felt more like an invitation than a challenge.

She walked Margaret to the door of her home, helped her over the wooden threshold, and then to a waiting Peter.

"Take care of yourself and the little one that is growing inside of you."

Margaret handed up the basket to Peter, who took it from her and placed it on the bench. She pulled herself up into the wagon and into Peter's strong arms. Margaret took the basket back and fluffed the tea towel over the biscuits. Peter looked down at the basket and tipped his hat knowingly at Emma. He knew what the basket held and his stomach started to growl in anticipation of their buttery goodness.

Emma knew exactly what she was going to do next. She was going to write Ellen, Jackson's sister, and invite her to come for a visit this Christmas. It seemed bold but she really wanted to see family this year, especially Jackson's.

Some call it providence… or the hand of God. A letter from Ellen preceded the arrival of Emma's letter to her.

Coming for a visit this Christmas. More details on my arrival will be forthcoming. I can't wait to see you, Emma. Get ready!
All my love — your sister, Ellen.

The making of the green velvet Christmas dress now had a new meaning and importance. Emma worked on it every day. Velvet is a heavy material and there were some days when Emma had to wait to work on it until late in the afternoon, when it was cooler.

That was okay because Emma had returned to her garden. This patch of dirt made her feel so alive and happy. She would go out early in the morning to pull the weeds that seemed to spring up from nowhere over-night. She'd pick things that were ready to eat, like squashes and beans, strawberries and corn. She had also planted her medicinal herbs and an assortment of flowers for cutting.

Peter helped her build a little fence around it to keep out the dogs and "other varmints," as he called them. At Emma's insistence he made a wooden sign for her garden that Emma painted and lettered with the words, "Time Began In A Garden."

Margaret made regular visits to Emma's home to learn about me-dicinal and culinary herbs and "other food things" that made Peter very happy. "What food things did you learn about today?" He was much more interested in this help from Emma than how to make a green velvet Christmas dress.

They bantered back and forth and it always came back to cookies, cakes and pies. Peter loved dessert. He asked her about her favorite fruit for a pie—apples, berries, peaches or cherries? She shared that the fruit was the best part of the pie to which he argued that it didn't matter what fruit was inside as long as the pie crust was buttery and flaky. "You know Emma, your apple pie, with its flaky and delicious crusts makes the fruit inside of it just a bit jealous." It was Peter's attempt at poetry and overpraise.

Through laughter she complimented him back, "Peter, you do have a way with words. Your Margaret is helping me make every pie that you are enjoying, so do give her some of the credit for them." He assured Emma that he did show gratitude to Margaret. He proudly stated that he and his pa did the dishes first to allow them time to savor her delicious desserts.

"We love to eat at home more than ever before. Between Margaret's new appetite and mine, we are packing on some winter pounds, just like the bears," and he stuck his belly out and patted it.

She couldn't help but laugh at Peter. He really was very funny and Emma enjoyed his humorous view of life as an expectant father. Finally, he picked up a huge pile of weeds and clippings for Emma. "Margaret tells me Jackson's sister, Ellen, is coming for a visit this Christmas."

"Yes, and I cannot wait to see her." Emma went on sharing about the plans she had for her visit and all the work yet to be done on the dress and preparations for her stay.

"Not to worry, Emma," Peter said. "I will fetch Aunt Ellen from the stage coach no matter what the weather is like."

Although she appreciated his desire to help, Emma knew someone else was going to need Peter a whole lot more. "Margaret and your son or daughter might need you more."

This thought made Peter tear up a little. He took off his hat, laid it over his heart, and pledged to be the best father ever. He also pledged to be there for Emma because he realized this was a very emotional visit with Jackson's sister coming all this way. Emma smiled at hearing him already affectionately call her "Aunt Ellen."

As she washed her hands under the pump she thought of things that Peter could do for his anxious feelings. She certainly understood his fidgetiness. Her son William had been a wiggle worm just like Peter. Short and meaningful tasks had helped him. She knew pulling weeds with her was good. She needed wood cut into smaller pieces for kindling, trimming some bushes, repairing the chicken coop, picking berries with the promise of a cobbler, and teaching him how to watercolor. She hoped that the tasks she taught him would help him settle down enough to concentrate for a good 20 to 30 minutes.

Emma was about to excuse herself from the garden, but before she left, she reminded Peter of the basket of fresh-picked things to go to Margaret. Peter grabbed the basket and examined its contents. He immediately began munching on a carrot, "Emma, I see some things in here that would make a delicious strawberry-rhubarb pie." And with that, he was off to do a few of his own farm chores with the hopes of a pie by the end of the day.

Emma returned inside to her work on the green velvet Christmas dress, as it had affectionately become known by Margaret, Mrs. McGeevy, Doc's wife, and some young girls that Emma was teaching how to sew and make pies. The making of the lining was tedious work, almost like making parts of the dress all over again. If this dress was going to endure time, as Emma hoped, the lining would be worth this effort. Plus, the dress needed a petticoat or two to make it stick out just a bit.

"You can't wear yards of heavy velvet without giving it some *pouf*," said Margaret. She loved saying the word pouf rather than petticoat. She would say it often and laugh each time she asked, "How far along is the pouf now?"

And Emma would say, "Let me show you its pouf-iness, Margaret."

Mrs. McGeevy had located more of the cream-colored fabric for the lining of the bodice and sleeves and other fabric for the petticoat. "It's a gift, Emma."

"You've already given me so much for this dress. How about some preserves and canned vegetables and peaches in trade?" bargained Emma.

"I would be honored to *sell* your goods at my mercantile." Mrs. McGeevy was a business woman and she knew Emma needed to add to her income from the fields. "I hear your garden is quite breathtaking and productive, and that it's in constant harvest."

"It is very giving. Time began in a garden, Mrs. McGeevy." She then added with a wink, "And God loves the color green, too."

Every night Emma would hang the dress up and stare at its beauty. Her visits to her family's grave was every couple of days now, instead of every day. She planted perennial flowers around the stone marker so there would always be something blooming. She could see their grave site if she stood in a certain place on the farm. When she looked there, she felt His peace now instead of the deep and painful ache.

As she gardened, her imagination would run off to what Jackson and the children were doing in Heaven. Today, she sensed her children were running in the fields of green with Jesus and all of the other children. Jackson was helping the Father, Son, and the Holy Spirit with mansion-building for the saints.

❧ 6 ❧

The fall that year was like no other fall Emma had ever experienced. The leaves turned amazing colors. The rains—so very needed—were refreshing. The wheat and oats that had been planted needed the rain, and so did the apple orchards.

Emma was invited to several homes for Thanksgiving. She decided to go to Peter and Margaret's home as Margaret was not feeling well that day. She needed to keep an eye on her and help with the dinner preparations. Peter, of course, welcomed Emma, knowing the results would be doubly delicious with Emma and Margaret cooking. As the evening wound down the elder Peter took out his fiddle and bow and played some tuneful and sweet music. Peter was his last child to be born. The father had sat in the rocking chair most of the evening, quietly rocking back and forth as if caught up in the memories of a lifetime of living, and many Thanksgivings. His wife had passed away years ago. Peter's brothers and sisters all lived elsewhere, and so the care of his father became Peter's and Margaret's responsibility and their joy.

Finally, it was time to say goodnight to everyone. Emma hugged Margaret and Peter, "Take care of each other and your little one as the day draws closer." She walked over to Peter, Sr., and bent down to hug him.

He whispered to her, "God will not forget what you have done for my children." Then he took Emma's hands in his and said, "These hands are healing hands, Emma. I know all about what God is going to do with the green velvet Christmas dress that you are making." He winked knowingly at Emma as if to say that he meant the words he'd just spoken.

The words took Emma by surprise. Her eyes filled with tears, and she gently kissed his forehead and whispered, "Thank you, Peter. I will receive this word and anticipate God's favor with this dress."

Margaret and Peter wondered about the exchange going on between the two of them, but knew it had to be good. Emma hugged each of them one more time and added: "Margaret, please have Peter fetch me if you feel the smallest something that you're not quite sure about later on this evening." Holding her arms around her growing child, Margaret nodded a yes to her.

Peter drove a quiet Emma home. She was deep in thought about his father's words to her: these hands are healing hands. Peter saw Emma into her home and helped her light lamps and stoke her fire. It was already a very cold night.

As he said his final goodnight he added, "Whatever my Pa said, count on it being a word of the Lord for you."

Alone again, she walked over to the mantle and took the picture of her family with her to her bedroom. She set it on her bedside table. She slipped on her nightgown and sat on the edge of her bed with her hands folded in prayer. She stared at Jackson, Emily and William for a long time. It was so different to spend a holiday without her family. She turned out her kerosene lamp and tucked herself down deep under the quilts, pulling her covers up tight around her neck. In a quiet whisper she prayed, *Father, I commit my ways and my hands unto you. Amen.*

Emma slept peacefully and soundly that night and woke up to the sounds of wood being chopped outside her front door. She opened the door to a happy Peter who said, "Good morning, Emma. It looks like snow today, so I am making sure you have plenty of wood for your stove and fireplace."

Emma's heart was happy over the thought of snow. "Thank you, Peter. I love it when it snows! And how is our Margaret doing this morning?"

"Well, I am hoping for just a light dusting of snow. Margaret is good and she is still asleep."

"Oh, it is so good to hear that, Peter. Let her sleep as much as she wants to right now. I'll be giving some gingerbread cookies a light dusting of snow sugar later on!"

"That kind of snow sounds delicious to me," said Peter with the sincere hope that several cookies would be his later.

"I thought you'd say that. And how are you doing today, Peter?" He always seemed fine but she wanted him to know she cared for him as well.

"Me? I am good, too. You'll let me know if you need a taster for your gingerbread cookies?"

She smiled to herself, remembering how Jackson and William often volunteered to be the tasters, especially if it was a sweet like a cookie or a pie. "There will be plenty for you to taste by about noon. Why don't Margaret and you come by for some lunch. The fresh air and a visit will do her good." Peter agreed and was off to tell Margaret.

By noon it was just starting to snow, and it made Christmas feel even closer. Emma welcomed Peter and Margaret into her warm home that smelled and looked like Christmas had already begun. That morning, Emma had opened the cedar chest to take out the hand-carved holy family that Jackson had made. She placed them on the mantle next to the picture of her family. She then gathered up some hay from the barn for baby Jesus, adding some fresh pine sprigs. It was a lovely little display. The three of them sat down to turkey soup, cornbread, gingerbread cookies, and coffee. They laughed and talked, and Emma gave her thoughts on possible names for their son or daughter. Peter and Margaret looked at each other.

"Emma, we already have the names for our son or daughter, and we want to know what you think of them," said Margaret, whose eyes were already filling up with tears.

Seeing the emotion welling up in his wife, Peter quickly said it: "If it's a boy we would like to name him Jackson, and if it's a girl, Emma."

Emma's eyes were now filling up with tears, which seemed to happen a great deal and whenever she spent time with these two. Margaret moved over to Emma's side to comfort her. She handed Peter's handkerchief to her and grabbed a tea towel for her own eyes.

"I hope these are happy tears?" asked Margaret. They had learned that Emma cried when she was sad and when she was happy. Sometimes they had to check.

"Yes, these are very happy tears! I'm just so honored, Peter and Margaret. Jackson would be, too. I so wish he were here so that he could have known you two. He'd love you just like I do."

Quickly a family hug was formed. That was another thing they loved about Emma's healing heart—she loved to hug people now. Some were taken aback by this kind of a gesture. Most people welcomed her hugs. Peter, Margaret, and Peter, Sr., surely did.

Emma enjoyed the daily company of Peter, Margaret, and Peter, Sr. Sharing this time of year with a young family expecting a child made the season a little less lonely and painful. They helped her laugh more and remember the joy of anticipating the birth of Christ.

Margaret and Peter welcomed any moment Emma opened up about one of her family stories. She shared how they would always add something new to their manger scene each day.

Carrying on the tradition, Emma had begun to draw in her sketch book, once again. While Peter did his watercolor work, she drew animals. As a result, her manger scene was filling up with tiny illustrations of God's creatures. There was a mouse, a squirrel, a pig, a cow, a donkey, a horse, two dogs, a cat, several lambs, and all kinds of birds. She loved drawing birds the most, especially sparrows. Each time they visited Emma Peter, Margaret, and Peter, Sr., went straight to the mantle to visit to see who had joined the manger scene. Emma's family joined the manger as well. She had placed them right next to Mary and Joseph. They were watching and anticipating His coming, too.

The dress was nearing its completion. Little things remained now, like yards and yards of hemming, the covered buttons for the cuffs and the waistband, and some very important embroidery. Emma had decided what she would embroider in the lining of the bodice. She had said it to herself and to the Lord as she finished the bodice: *Lord, I will wear this dress on the day when sorrow is no more.*

Margaret came for a short visit as she was feeling very tired. She sat down and joined Emma for more hemming of the pouf. She still giggled every time she heard the word. She told Emma that being with her helped pass this anxious time. Waiting for the baby to be born was so hard for both of them, but maybe more so for Peter.

"He's run out of things to prepare, make, mend, tend, fix, stain, or paint. As you well know, he's extra fidgety and nervous!" Margaret stood up and stretched. Emma eyed her, thinking she looked very ready to give birth. Holding her abdomen, Margaret said, "I am more achy and heavy today. My lower back hurts something awful. Nothing sounds good to eat."

"Did you eat anything today?" Emma inquired like a doting mother. She went to the stove and started to heat up the soup she'd had the night before. "Chicken and rice soup. How does that sound?"

"Tolerable," Margaret replied as she leaned against the fireplace, one hand on the small of her back. And then it happened. Margaret's water broke.

Emma pulled one of the dining room chairs over to her. "I'll take you home right now. Can you sit down on this chair, Margaret, while I--"

Interrupting her she snapped, "No I can't, Emma! I'm afraid to sit down!"

"Then let's stand. You lean on the mantle and here's the chair right next to you now, if you need it. I'm going to get my things very quickly because you are having your baby today, Margaret!" Emma's voice was calm and joyous at the same time. It seemed to eclipse Margaret's pain for a few seconds.

"I am?'"

"Yes, you are. Today."

Emma rushed about the room, scooping up the things that Margaret had brought with her along with the things she'd need, thinking that it might be a long night. Babies take their time.

"Emma! Help!" Margaret's voice was filled with pain and a little bit of fear after the last contraction. "Peter said he'd be back here by now. Why isn't he here yet?" she winced.

"I will hitch up old Luke and take you to your home, myself."

"But what about the *pouf*?" asked Margaret in a quivering voice.

"The pouf can wait!" This statement made them both laugh.

Emma quickly took the soup off of the stove, blew out the lamplights, and took one last look around her home for anything else that she'd need. She gently turned Margaret around and helped her to lean on the table while she ran to the bedroom. She returned with the quilt she had made for Margaret's and Peter's baby and gently stuffed it into her basket. She tightly wrapped Margaret's shawl around her shoulders.

As Emma opened the door they saw Peter on his rig. In all of the excitement he'd arrived and was waiting patiently in the snow.

The second he saw them struggling he knew what was going on. He bounded off of the rig and ran to the both of them. He gently picked up Margaret and placed her in the wagon. He then helped Emma up, who was struggling with several baskets.

"What's all of this, food?"

"No, Peter. It's things that we'll need for your baby's birth. You're going to become a father today or tonight!"

Peter's heart leapt and he gently maneuvered the horse and wagon down the road, not wanting to make the ride difficult for his Margaret. In moments they were at their farm. Once again, Peter picked Margaret up and took her into their bedroom. Placing her ever so gently on the bed he said, "I love you, Margaret." Returning to the living room he announced excitedly, "I'm going to go get Doc, Pa! You stay here and take good care of Margaret and Emma."

Emma added as Peter was about to take off, "Tell Doc things seem to be hurrying along here."

Peter, Sr., was immediately up and stoking the fire now. "What can I do to help, Emma? Boil some water?"

"For tea, yes. Most important, I need you to pray, Peter," said Emma. "Pray those big fatherly prayers of yours for Margaret and your grandchild."

"I can do that." He poked the logs in the fireplace and took his Bible from the mantle.

Emma returned to Margaret, who had slipped out of her dress, shoes and stockings.

"How is the pain now?"

"Tolerable but regular. It is coming and going just like you said it would," she added, as Emma helped her put on her dressing gown.

"That's perfect," said Emma.

"Perfect—perfect pain?!"

Using her most reassuring voice, Emma said, "No, but we do want regular contractions. Make sure you're breathing through each one just like we practiced, Margaret. Remember?"

Margaret shook her head yes and breathed and grimaced through a small contraction.

"Will you get me a pair of Peter's socks? My feet are freezing. Right in the top drawer of the dresser." Emma found a pair of woolen socks and put them on Margaret's feet. "A little big, don't you think?" And they both laughed at the sight of Margaret's feet in those floppy woolen socks.

"They feel so good." And with another contraction, she shrieked loudly, "Please Peter, hurry!"

Peter, Sr., heard his name as Margaret's screeched through the pain, and was at the bedroom door in seconds. "What can I do?"

Emma instructed him to watch the clock and time his daughter's contractions. He assured Emma that he knew how to do this from his own children's births. He returned to the fire, put another log on it, filled the tea kettle with water, and placed it on the back burner. Then he sat in the rocking chair, staring at his silver pocket watch and praying.

Peter and Doc finally arrived. It was now dark and a little icy out, so the travel to the farm was slower than they had both hoped. "How is she doing?" asked Doc.

"She's tolerating the pain but very uncomfortable," said Emma as Doc followed her into the bedroom.

Peter and his father discussed making something for supper and busied themselves in the kitchen. Peter, Sr., took this opportunity to reassure his son that birth was something that couldn't be hurried. "In fact, your poor Mother was in labor for more than a day with you, Peter. You were a bit of a slow poke." This sounded funny to Peter as he was never slow about anything. Ever.

More time passed and after several cups of tea Peter said, "I can't take this waiting any longer, Pa! I'm going to go see my wife."

He went to the bedroom door and asked if he could see Margaret. "Please, Doc, for just a minute," he pleaded.

"Of course, you can see her. She's resting between contractions right now. She is okay, Peter, but very tired." Doc had seen plenty of anxious dads but Peter was the most anxious one in a long time.

"Emma, let's get ourselves a cup of tea."

Peter tiptoed in and sat on the edge of the bed next to his wife. He gently took her hand in his. He stared at her as she looked so very peaceful and beautiful to him. Sensing his presence, she opened her eyes and looked at her husband. "How are you doing, Peter?"

"I am doing good. Pa is doing good. The cows are doing good, too. They're all milked. The chickens even laid a few extra eggs which I brought in. The wood is chopped and loaded up next to the door. The snow stopped falling but it's very cold outside." Margaret then squeezed his hand tightly through another contraction and it stopped his nervous chatter.

Her grip was very strong, and it hurt him a little bit. He felt helpless as he watched her breathe through the contraction, then he felt her loosen her grip on his hand. He wished there was a way to trade places. He had never seen his wife in pain like this before. He felt brave and helpless and small, all at the same time.

"Margaret?"

"Yes, Peter?"

"I love you."

"I love you, too, Peter. "

"Margaret, together, we will love our child in a way that we've never known love before. Pa just told me that. He said, 'You two will be changed forever, once you are parents.' I figure the best parts of you and me are about to rise to the top like the cream on a bucket of Becky's fresh milk."

This made Margaret laugh. "Peter, you are so funny!"

"That didn't come out quite the way I hoped it would," and he laughed with her.

Doc, Emma, and Peter, Sr., loved the sound of the laughter coming from that room.

"Peter!" Margaret screamed his name and squeezed his hand again. Peter winced as her grip hurt much more than the last time. Doc and Emma returned to the room and Peter slipped back to his Pa's side.

"I have an idea!" Emma said, raising her voice loudly so Peter and his father could hear her speak. "We'll sing through the contractions with you, Margaret." It seemed like an odd idea from the next room, but they kept listening. Doc agreed that this was a great idea. It would help Margaret with her breathing during the next part of her labor.

"Next part?" asked Margaret with an uneasiness in her voice.

"Yes, it's almost time to push, Margaret," said Doc.

"Well, I can't think of any Christmas hymns that I want to sing right now." Just then Pa began to play on his violin, *What Child Is This?*

Everyone began to sing, including Doc. It was very calming for Margaret, who did her best to sing and breathe through the pain. After the last notes of the song, Margaret said, "Doc, I think I need to push now."

Doc and Emma hurriedly made adjustments in the room, placing things where they needed them to be, and then they took positions at the head and the foot of Margaret.

"We're ready for the next song, Pa," said Doc loudly. Peter's father then began to play "*Silent Night*." After singing the song several times, the most glorious music one would ever want to hear filled the room—the cry of a newborn baby. Peter and his Father peeked in the room, anxious to hear if it was a Jackson or an Emma.

"One moment, please," said Emma. "And Peter, please scramble some eggs for all of us. And make some coffee, too?"

It was way after supper time, almost midnight. Breakfast sounded good to everyone so Peter and his father went to work. The smell of bacon frying, scrambled eggs, toasted bread, and coffee filled their home. Just as they finished, Doc asked Peter and his father to step into the room.

Like two small children awaiting a Christmas surprise, they stepped into the room quietly. There in the middle of the large featherbed, sitting up and looking the most beautiful she had ever looked in all her life was Margaret, holding little Emma Joy.

Peter moved in close to his wife. Margaret held out her arms filled with God's glorious goodness and said, "Here's your little girl, Emma Joy. And here is your papa, Emma Joy."

Peter held his daughter and a surge of love, protection, and possession took over his heart, coupled with an utter feeling of helplessness. He'd never felt such a conflict of emotions in all of his life!

"She's so small," was all he could muster along with "I love you, Emma Joy." Peter motioned his father to step closer and get a good look at his new granddaughter.

"She's a little beauty, Margaret." The words came in a whisper with a voice cracking from emotion and pride.

"Thank you, Pa. She has dark hair like your side of the family."

In a gentle voice, he added, "And thank you Lord that she has your nose, Margaret. Oh, hello little Emma Joy. We're all so glad that you are here!"

"Oh Doc, thank you so much," said Peter, Sr.

"We couldn't have done it without Emma's help, right Margaret?" Doc gestured to Emma. Everyone turned their gaze to the woman who had become so dear to all of them. She tried to fade into the wooden boards of the wall, overcome with emotion by this birth. She was a mess—crying and sobbing for the joy, for the sadness, for the grace, the love and the mercy of God's unfailing love, and for this dear family that she had come to love as if they were of her own flesh and blood. She walked over and placed her arms around Peter and his father, "I'm embarrassed to say this, but I am quite undone by you, little Miss Emma Joy. Her middle name is just perfect."

"It was Pa's idea. He said her middle name should be Joy for that is what she will bring into this world."

"She sure has," Emma said as she wiped tears of joy with her apron. "You've captured all of our hearts, little one."

Peter, Sr., brought back his fiddle and bow and began to play, "*Joy To The World.*"

Can you dance to a Christmas hymn? This family did. They danced through all four verses. Such joy had never filled a room before. And Emma Joy went right to sleep with all that noise.

7

Emma had spent the last several weeks putting finishing touches on the dress and helping Margaret with Emma Joy. It is such a delight for her to see parenting from this vantage point.

She busied herself with food for Ellen's visit and a little more decorating. Ellen would arrive today or tomorrow depending upon the weather. Memories of her family's many Christmases could bring joy and sorrow, all in the same moment. Every now and then, their loss and absence at this special time of year would weigh her down and she would feel like staying in bed. And she did just that on one of those days.

Emma had returned to church. She now sat with Peter, Sr., Peter, Margaret and Emma Joy just as she had said she would. Everyone was so happy to see Emma. She'd been deeply missed. She was one of those kinds of people that didn't cause you to go the other way when you saw them coming. Instead, you drew close to her. She made you feel like your story mattered more than hers did.

Emma had bought Christmas gifts for her family. It gave her an odd kind of comfort to buy a little something for each one of them. She had found just the right big-girl doll for Emily, a caboose for William's train, a knife for Jackson, and for Ellen, her husband's mother's combs.

Every year, Emma wrote a Christmas poem. These poems were told to her family first, and then on Christmas Eve, after dinner. She saved all her poetry in a leather-bound book that Jackson had made. It was also the place of her sketches, Bible verses, and the things God had told her. She now called it *My Book Of Remembering.* This book was how she traced God's hand in her life. This year, if she could tell it through the tears, she planned to share her Christmas poem with Ellen. It was called, *Your Face,* and she had finished it just a few days ago.

YOUR FACE

Did you cry the day your Son left Home for all of us on earth?

Did you know the shepherds and the Kings would celebrate His birth?

Of course, you did, oh Mighty God, you planned it bit by bit,

You cried, you laughed, you thought of us so lacking in Your wit.

For royal robes exchanged that night for cotton swaddling clothes,

Would begin the walk of Calvary to redeem our long-lost souls.

I cried the day you called them home from this whirling place called earth.

How could you Lord—my beloved husband and the children I had birthed.

And then I saw You one dark night Your glistening eyes so pained,

You felt it, too. You knew it well, the day your Son we gained.

So dear Mighty God who pinned the stars and hung the moon in place,

Please know I love You more today for I have seen Your face.

Ellen's arrival was accompanied by another light snowfall. Peter, true to his word, stopped by to tell Emma that he was leaving to go get her.

"Please help Ellen off of your wagon and to my door when you return. I will have a special surprise for her when I open the door."

"Can I see it, too? I think I know what it is, Emma."

"Later on, Peter. We will come see all of you on Christmas evening."

"I think I know what it is, Emma," he said with an annoying grin.

There were times when Peter felt more like the exasperating little brother that she'd never had, and this was one of them. "Peter, please go get my sister for me!"

"I am on my way, right now, Emma. And everyone is fine at home," he pouted, missing Emma's personal attention during instructions about her sister-in-law.

Emma prepared for Ellen's arrival. She had finished the last of the embroidery in the lining of the bodice that morning. She dressed slowly, from head to toe, in the green velvet Christmas dress. Her ensemble was completed by a hat made with some of the velvet and special beading, embroidery, and feathers that Mrs. McGeevy helped her find. Before she was married Mrs. McGeevy had been a milliner. She was delighted to make a personal contribution to the green velvet Christmas dress. It was the fanciest hat Emma had ever worn in her life.

After tucking a lavender scented hankie into her sleeve, Emma sat down in her rocking chair to wait for Ellen. She watched as light snow began to fall, making everything outside look like a Currier and Ives lithograph. She hoped it wouldn't delay Ellen's arrival. She stood up (which was a little bit of a challenge in the green velvet Christmas dress) and took off one of her gloves to place a few more logs on the fire to warm her home for her guest.

Then, she heard the Christmas bells tied to Peter's rig. Peter attached a set of handsome brass bells to the horse's harnesses every holiday. They provided a musical announcement each time he came with his rig to her home. Emma loved hearing them and this time they heralded the arrival of her Ellen dearest!

Emma's heart was beating very fast now. She peeked out the window and saw Peter helping Ellen off of the wagon. He handed her a tapestry bag and a suitcase. She could hear them climb the step to her porch, stomping and dusting off the snow that had fallen on them.

He said loudly so Emma could hear through the door: "I need to be on my way. Goodbye, Aunt Ellen. We will see you tomorrow evening. Merry Christmas until then!"

He tipped his hat and was about to go, as he'd promised, when Ellen touched his arm and said, "Thank you so much, Peter. You're everything Emma described and more."

"I am? Why thank you, Aunt Ellen!" He then tipped his hat one more time, hustled onto the wagon, whistled to his horses, and was on his way.

Ellen then knocked on the door and said, "Emma, it's me!" The door opened and what she saw took her breath away.

"Merry Christmas, Ellen dearest!"

Emma was wearing the green velvet Christmas dress, a matching hat, black silk gloves, and black shiny boots, with a smart-looking reticule at her wrist. To Ellen she looked like a portrait from a page of *Peterson's Magazine*.

Emma and Ellen fell into each other's arms and laughed for joy, and then cried for the meaning of the visit. They held on to each other for several minutes, not wanting to be the first to let go.

Then Ellen took a few steps away from Emma. She wanted to drink in every aspect of Emma in this dress. "Let me have a good look at you, Emma Grace Harris. This dress is just a work of elegance and beauty. Turn please." Emma did. She turned a full circle as tears continued to fill Ellen's eyes. She gushed over the next words, "Jackson and the children would be so proud of what you have made."

"They are," added Emma with a special confidence. "As sure as you and I are standing here, I am certain they are proud of me today."

Ellen hugged Emma once again. "I wanted to be here with you, Emma." She took out her hanky and began to really cry. Tears of grief flowed that had been saved for months.

Emma guided her to the small settee and wrapped her arms around her. "I know you did, dear Ellen. I know you did. It all happened so very quickly for us."

"It did. And then the weather, and..."

"Oh, Ellen dearest, I do not want this visit to be about what you didn't do for us. You loved your brother and you loved your niece and nephew. And I know your prayers lifted me to a higher place—a better place—where I could see the face of God. He was with me in ways I do know; and in ways I will not know until I meet Him face to face." Emma took Ellen's hands in hers. "Your brother loved you dearly. Before his death, we spoke of your next visit that he hoped would be at Christmas. He told me he wanted me to take you to his grave and give you something very special."

Ellen's curiosity was piqued about the gift, but not as much as her appetite. It had been almost two days of travel by train and then a bumpy stage coach.

"We'll go to their graves tomorrow," Emma promised. "You must be famished."

"I am and it all smells so delicious," Ellen replied, spying the table brimming with family favorites.

"Yes, it's all for you," Emma laughed. But first I have a favor to ask of you. I want you to put on the green velvet Christmas dress," she said with a knowing smile.

"Really?" Surprise and curiosity lifted Ellen's voice.

"It fits everyone who tries it on."

Ellen agreed and it did. The green velvet Christmas dress fit her, too! Ellen reached for her handkerchief and began blotting her eyes, once again. "I saw the writing in the lining—*Worn on the day when sorrow was no more.* This is that day isn't it, Emma?"

"Yes, it is. That's what today feels like for me. Having you here with me, dear Ellen, has brought joy and family into my home once again. Thank you for coming all this way for me."

The next day, Emma and Ellen trudged through several inches of fresh snow to the graves of Jackson, Emily, and William. Emma had put on the green velvet Christmas dress again. She had decided she was going to wear it all day. Once they reached the graves, Emma said, "I have your Christmas gift from Jackson." She reached inside her purse and handed Ellen a box tied with a scrap of green velvet. "Ellen, these hair combs belonged to your mother."

"I don't think I'll ever stop crying." Ellen's eyes filled with tears once again, remembering that her mother and Jackson were together now in Heaven. "Oh, I remember these." They were still in the original box. It was the sweetest gift and gesture she had ever received. They had been a wedding gift to Emma from Jackson's mother. Giving them to Ellen was like returning a family treasure back to its owner. Ellen then held them to her chest, realizing it was the last gift from her brother that she would ever receive.

Emma had brought a huge bouquet of pine and hawthorn berry sprigs tied up with another long scrap of the green velvet. She handed them to Ellen, who gently laid them on her loved one's graves. Ellen did the same thing Emma had done upon seeing their names engraved in stone: she traced each name with her fingers and said the prayer out loud.

May the Lord watch between me and thee, while we are absent one from another.

They stood in silence for a long time after that, drinking in the beauty of winter's white robes at this final resting place of Emma's and Ellen's family. They prayed together for a while before they began to get cold. The sun was starting to go down and evening was approaching. Emma knew that Ellen might need a bit of time to rest and freshen up before heading to their Christmas evening with Peter, Margaret, Pa, and Emma Joy. Emma couldn't wait to see everyone's expressions when they opened the door and she stood before them in the dress.

Emma, christmas Day 1880.
worn on the day when sorrow
was no more.

8

Years passed. Emma never remarried. There was many a widower that eyed the attractive Emma, but her heart would always belong to Jackson. She continued to teach little girls how to sew, cook, and bake. She went away to Teachers College—Mary Baldwin College. After returning, she taught in town. She loved teaching children of all ages, especially young teens. They were on the edge of life and she encouraged many of them to pursue college.

She also became fascinated with the country of China and its people. More and more women were being given permission to do missionary work overseas. Emma wrote to a missionary society to ask if she could join their work as a teacher. She knew this meant selling the farm, her home of nearly 20 years. She decided to sell it to Margaret and Peter, with the promise that a portion of its crop's sales would be used for Emma Joy's college tuition. Not knowing what lay ahead, she sent the green velvet Christmas dress to Ellen. She knew it would be kept safe and passed on in her family.

Dear Ellen,
The farm is sold to Peter and Margaret. Isn't that wonderful?

My things are packed. I will be leaving for China shortly. I am hoping your promise is still true about having a place to stay in Chicago. I am counting on this kindness when I return to the United States. Please don't be frightened or sad about me heading to China. Be happy for me, dearest Ellen. The Lord is taking me on a wonderful adventure. I can't wait to see what He has in store for me there.

I will never forget that Christmas we spent together following Jackson's and the children's passing. I will always remember your face when I greeted you at the door in "the green velvet Christmas dress," as it was affectionally named by Margaret.

That night I slowly dressed, from head to toe, and sat in my rocking chair wait-ing for your arrival. The look on your face when I said, "Merry Christmas, Ellen dearest!" set us both to laughing and crying at the same time. Remember? Then, you heard about the making of the green velvet Christmas dress and of how making the dress kept me alive, despite the tremendous sorrow and great darkness that followed their deaths. Oh, how I loved that the dress fit you, too. That was such a wonderful Christmas, dear Ellen. You were an important part of the healing of my desperate soul. Your prayers made all of the difference in my healing. Thank you for coming all that way for me.

I am leaving my dress to your safekeeping.

Ellen, this green velvet Christmas dress is destined for more. I had the strongest feeling while making it that there was a goodness in this green velvet that would outlast me. Actually, it was Mrs. McGeevy, from the mercantile, who said it first. Every young and older woman that has tried it on manages to slip into its green goodness. It fits them, too. Just like it fit you! I find that so amazing. Don't you, Ellen?

May I beg you to pass it on to your children, and to ask them to pass it on to someone in their family? Only God knows where it will finally end up, but I know it will carry a story with what I embroidered in the lining in 1880.

I am so grateful that God made us sisters. I've never thought of you as my sister-in-law, only my beloved sister. Oh, how your life has been pressed deeply into mine by our good Lord.

Remember, always, that your name means 'beautiful woman,' Ellen. Even though our gray hair and wrinkles betray our age and the years that we've lived upon this earth, you remain a beautiful gift from God for all that know you. Live that truth, as this world changes much too quickly for both of us.

I will always love you. The Lord watch between me and thee while we are absent one from another.

Emma Grace Harris

Emma and Ellen wrote many letters and cards while Emma was overseas. Ellen saved every one of them. True to her word, Ellen kept the green velvet Christmas dress safely tucked away in the chest that her brother had made. It was sent to Ellen along with the hand-carved nativity pieces when Emma's farm was sold. It made perfect sense to place the dress in the chest along with all of the correspondence from years of family and a deep sister-friendship.

After Ellen passed, her daughter, Beth, took the cedar-lined chest and the dress when her mother's things were divided up. This eldest daughter tried on the dress one evening when she was feeling particularly sad and lonely for her mother's arms and her nearness. And the dress fit Beth, too.

9

The green velvet dress was safely kept in the cedar chest, taken out on special occasions and whenever the story was shared of how it came to be the green velvet Christmas dress. When Beth passed away, the cedar chest and the dress went to her only daughter, Anah, Ellen's granddaughter.

As it did everyone else, the dress fit Anah, too. She loved to tell the story of her grandmother's and great aunt's relationship. She did a show-and-tell when she told it. She'd say with a smile, "I want to stop the story of their lives right now and show you something. I'll be right back." She'd disappear to her bedroom (sometimes followed by a female friend) and open up the cedar chest at the end of her bed. She'd slip into the dress's green goodness, come back and model it for the adoring listeners. The first thing they wanted to do is feel the velvet and then see the embroidered words. In mixed company, she'd excuse herself again, change back into her clothes, and return with the dress. In the company of just women, she'd ask one of them to help her by unbuttoning a few of the dress's covered buttons, so that she could reveal where Emma had placed her embroidery. It was where one's right back shoulder would be if one was wearing the dress. That's where Emma had felt God's hand and His joy over her the day she began the creation of the green velvet Christmas dress.

Anah and her family ended up moving to California in 1944. One of their two small moving vans was broken into while spending the night in a motel in Arizona. Many things were stolen.

Now, there are many things that we can do without. This kind of tragedy reveals to us the things that are easily replaced, unneeded, even unnecessary in our lives. Then there are those things that make our hearts sick when they are stolen from us. Of all the things to steal—an old chest with a velvet dress, and dozens of letters and cards tucked away inside of it. Anah and her husband filed paperwork for their stolen items and did their own personal searching for the chest and the green velvet Christmas dress. Sadly, they never found them.

❧ RACHEL ❦

It was hot Saturday morning in July of 1945. A young military wife stationed in Long Beach, California, was doing what she loved to do on Saturdays. She had grabbed breakfast at the local diner and spent her morning combing through a few thrift stores and second hand shops. She called it treasure hunting. Her best friend, Vivian, called it junking.

But this was not junk. No, Rachel thought it was the find of the lifetime. It was an old hand-carved, cedar-lined chest. With curiosity she lifted the lid to see if anything was inside. There were wonderful things to be found by looking inside old chests, trunks, and the drawers of dressers and desks. To her joy and surprise, wrapped in fragile tissues and brown paper was a lovely green velvet dress. She wanted to take it out and try it on right then and there. Instead she asked Stan, the owner of the thrift store, if she could have the chest and dress inside of it. He sized up the contents quickly and said, "Mrs. Sergeant, keep it. It's yours."

Rachel was thrilled and wanted to tell him she was certain it was real velvet but decided Stan probably wouldn't have cared if it was. To him things were business transactions, bargains, and sales. He did love it when his customers asked him if he would take less for something at Stan's Bargains & Treasures. "What are you going to do with that old dress? It's very out of date."

Rachel laughed as she held it up over her figure. "True, but I know how to sew, and my sailor is coming home from the war soon. I'm going to make a welcome home dress with it."

Stan was Italian and had been around the block a time or two. Nothing was new to him in dealing with old items, but he was in one of his generous moods. "Then today is your lucky day for old things, Mrs. Sergeant! You get an old chest and an old dress."

"It's not luck, Stan," Rachel told him.

"Yes, I know. Jesus, Mary, and Joseph, and the three wise men are looking after you." He appreciated her as a customer but not all the talk about God helping her with every little thing in her life. It was boring to him, unless it meant selling something like a nativity set, a crucifix, or a picture of a saint or the pope.

"It's God, Stan. He's the one who has been looking after me while my husband has been in the war. Why don't you come to church with Vivian and me tomorrow? It is your day off. We'll be back for the trunk later today. I'm bringing you cookies, Stan, in exchange for the green velvet dress. Think about it."

Stan knew she was going to ask him to go to church when she returned. His polite refusals never stopped Rachel from asking. "You probably think your cookies will convince me to go to church with you," he said as he handed her the receipt that read "Old cedar chest and free green velvet dress." He placed a red sold sticker on the chest and moved it to the front of the shop, near his counter.

"You can't blame a Protestant for trying, can you, Stan?"

"Well no I can't. But I'm Catholic today."

Rachel and Vivian were next-door neighbors on the base and the best of friends. Their husbands were in the navy and had shipped out for World War II on the same day. They shared everything. Rachel had a sewing machine; Vivian had a station wagon. Rachel could cook just about anything because she'd learned how from her father, who owned a restaurant. Vivian could fix just about any car issue as she'd grown up with mechanic for a father, plus four brothers. Rachel was known as "the rationing chef of Bungalow 12." Vivian was often referred to as "Bungalow 11's cab and repair service." Between the two of them, you could pick up a ride, get your oil changed, a shirt or skirt mended, and a tummy filled. The only hitch: you might have to go to church with these two. Not a bad deal, really. Lunch might follow the service.

They returned to Stan's Bargains & Treasures to load the chest into Vivian's car. Try as they did, Stan made no promises about going to church the next day. He did want to know how Rachel had gotten hold of butter, eggs, and sugar to make him the most delicious snickerdoodle cookies he had ever tasted. And he laughed at several of Vivian's jokes. "Oh, Vivian, you need to stop making me laugh, or I will be choking on a snickerdoodle; and it will be all your fault," said Stan as he lifted the chest into the back of her station wagon.

"Well, we wouldn't want to be responsible for that, Stan-the-Thrift-Store-Man. See you at church. It's on the corner of Fifth Street and Diamond Lane," and Vivian and Rachel drove away before Stan could make up an excuse.

Rachel had Vivian walk backward up the stairs with her end of the chest, so she could guide her into the bungalow. "Easy does it, Rachel."

"Are we almost there?"

"Yes, just turn it around so I can unlock the door." Once inside, Vivian and Rachel lowered the chest to the ground. Vivian sat on top of it, fanning herself with the lid from a box of ornaments. "It's a sturdy chest, too." She then began singing, "I'm dreaming of a white Christmas," to add to the festive mood.

It wasn't just hot that day; it was sticky, too. But Rachel's tiny living room looked like Christmas was days away with boxes of holiday things spread about. "Those two words don't seem to go together – 'Christmas' and 'July'," said Vivian.

"Oh, but they do for me and it's all for Ronnie!" She handed her a glass of iced tea which Vivian applied to her forehead because of its icy contents.

"So, did you find any treasures inside this old chest?"

Rachel pulled Vivian up off of the chest so that she could open it up and show her the dress.

Just then the phone rang.

"It's Ronnie, Viv!" she said dropping her abruptly back down onto the chest.

This was the call Rachel had been waiting for. Hopefully her husband's details on the timing of his return home would be a part of this phone call. Rachel picked up the phone and with love and great affection she said, "Ronnie!"

Her face fell: "Oh hello, Mother." She began listening to how her mother had tried calling her several times earlier in the day, with no answer. She was worried that something might have happened to her way out there in California.

"I'm fine, Mother," she said feeling annoyed that her mother still worried about her being in another state after all these years. "I was out and busy getting things ready for Ronnie's homecoming."

Vivian made a funny face at her and mouthed, "Should I go?" to which Rachel motioned back to her to wait. Now her mom was on to another complaint. "No, I'm not disappointed that you called me, Mother. I just thought you were Ronnie. I'm expecting a call from him today about his return home. Just a minute Mama. I need to say goodbye to Viv. Yes, I'll tell her hello for you."

Rachel and Vivian hugged one another as they always did when they parted company. With both of their husbands in the Navy and being from out of state, their friendship was based on survival and staving off the loneliness and worry that accompanied life on a military base during a major world war.

Vivian whispered, "Don't forget we're volunteering at the USO tonight. I can't wait to taste your treats," and acted like someone ravenously hungry.

Rachel threw back at her: "Well, I can't wait to see you do the Lindy Hop again!" Vivian danced a few steps of the Lindy with Rachel which made her drop the phone she'd been holding. She picked it up quickly, "Sorry, Mama. Just give me one more second."

She hugged Vivian again. "They're really coming home, Viv." They both teared up, and Vivian pulled herself together and Lindy Hopped her way out the door and over to her apartment.

Rachel told her mother all about the cedar-lined chest that she had discovered at the thrift store in town. Her mother chided her about spending money, but Rachel assured that the chest was a steal. She juggled the phone as she opened the lid and pulled out the green velvet dress. She told her mother of her plans to make a smart and sophisticated welcome home dress from the yards of velvet in the old garment. Rachel flipped on the electric fan as she assured her mother, "Yes, I know it's hot in California, Mama. But we're going to have Christmas in July, and I am going to wear a green velvet dress to welcome my husband home! We've missed several Christmases already, and we are going to catch up and celebrate big time!"

Rachel told her mother about the lining in the dress and the embroidered saying that she found in the dress: *Emma, Christmas Day 1880. Worn on the day when sorrow was no more.*

"Isn't that lovely, Mama? Can you imagine the story this woman must have gone through to stitch that into the lining of her dress?" She declared that she was going to do the very same thing when she reused the lining for the dress she would make. Her mother inquired about what she would embroider, and she told her, "Ready, Mama? *Rachel 1945. Grateful to be grateful.*"

Her mother was silent except for the obvious sniffles on the other end of the phone. "Mama, are you all right? I know, it's no Hallmark card, but it's how I truly feel."

Her mother told her it was the most beautiful thing she had heard all day. Rachel assured her that she'd be the first one she called when she found out about her husband's return home. She hung up the phone hoping she hadn't missed an opportunity to talk to her husband. He only had so many chances to use a phone as everyone else needed to make a call, too.

Rachel walked over to her dressing mirror and held the dress up over her figure. Tossing the sleeves over her shoulders, she folded the dress at the waist and hiked up the skirt to reveal her legs. "Yes, this will work. It's going to be lovely." She then hobbled over to her dresser where there was a burlwood framed photo of her husband. "Hurry home, my love."

The green velvet dress Rachel wore was gorgeous and yes, it surprised her sailor. None of the other wives or girlfriends were wearing a green velvet evening dress with a matching velvet stole.

Rachel and Ronnie had three children, all sons. Their family eventually moved to Chicago, where Ronnie continued to serve at the Great

Lakes Naval Training Center, very close to where Rachel's parents lived. It was good to be close to family while raising their boys.

It took her more time than expected to finish college, but Rachel became a teacher at a local high school. She was one of the last of an almost unheard-of breed of educators called "home economics teachers." She taught teenage girls and boys how to cook, sew, make a budget, keep a checkbook balanced, fill out tax forms, and how to change a tire and the oil in their cars thanks to her best friend. "Someday, you'll need to know how to do this. I learned how from my best friend, Vivian Styles, during World War II."

Surprising to all who knew and loved her, Rachel passed away in her early sixties after a long battle with cancer. She was remembered by Ronnie as the most attractive woman he'd ever seen that very hot day in July of 1945. "The minute I stepped off the ship, I spotted her. She had told me she'd be wearing green, but I was not expecting such a knockout of a dress. She'd sewn it all by herself. Then we went directly home to a house decorated with holiday cheer and a delicious Christmas meal. It was the best food I'd eaten since I'd shipped out."

After Rachel passed away her dress was worn by her three granddaughters. They loved dressing up in the green velvet homecoming dress that welcomed their grandpop home from the war. They would trace their fingers over the words she'd stitched into the lining of her dress every time they wore it or handled it. It was a common phrase that Rachel used all of her life, right up to her final breath: "I'm so grateful to be grateful."

It was last worn by the eldest granddaughter, Jennifer, when she played Adelaide in her high school's musical production of *Guys and Dolls*. She wanted to keep the dress, and everyone agreed that she looked the most like her Grandma Ray-Ray when she wore it. For years it was scooted to the back of her closet with all the other things she didn't wear anymore.

made by Rachel for
christmas in July 1945.
Grateful to be grateful

However, not everyone appreciates the importance of that one-of-a-kind keepsake of an outfit. We know, but they don't know its value beyond compare. The green velvet dress was separated from Jennifer's things after she moved into an apartment with some friends. She looked for it on a lonely Saturday when she was missing her Grandma Ray-Ray. (She always felt better when she tried it on.) Jennifer panicked when she couldn't find it, and accused her roommates of borrowing it without her permission to which they complained, "That old thing? Who'd want to wear that? Not us!"

She racked her brain about when she had worn it last. Did someone borrow it for Halloween? Had she taken it home? No one had seen the dress since her high school musical performance. Jennifer prayed for its return, but it was gone. All she had was the memory of wearing it and some photographs. However, no one could ever remove the story of a life well lived, the meaning behind the making of the green velvet welcome home dress, and a very special Christmas in July of 1945 at the end of World War II.

❖ LAUREL & BARB ❖

The low hum of a boombox played Christmas music as Laurel ripped through the seam to separate two large pieces of fabric. She loved when they came apart so quickly and easily. She stood up, making the move of a dancer as Bing Crosby crooned "White Christmas" in the work room. Laurel poured her special throat tea into a floral tea cup that reminded her of spring and not Christmas.

"Oh please, no snow today or I will really be depressed." Laurel pulled out her CD of "The Nutcracker" and placed it in the boombox. The overture swelled, and as she did a few pas de bourrée to its opening strains she noticed a note from Barb taped to a box:

Dear Laurel,

Madame Angelika prefers the color green over red. I have scoured some of my favorite places for remnants and vintage material. Then I found these green pieces down in the bowels of our theater. Boy, is it scary down there! Do NOT go down there alone, like I did last night.

See if any of them will work for her jacket. I'll call you when I get off the train.

Laurel lifted the lid of the plastic bin and began sifting through the material. Then she found it among the many green pieces: It was a stunning green velvet evening dress. "Wait, this is real velvet, Barb, and someone sure knew how to sew. It's quite attractive."

Just then the phone rang. Laurel knew it had to be Barb. She cleared her throat and answered in a peppy voice: "Chicago's best costumers! Laurel speaking. Hey there, hello Barb!" She listened to Barb's short lecture on department phone etiquette and interrupted her. "Yes, I know, I know. I don't answer the phone like that. I usually say, ' Rand Theater, Costume Department. This is Laurel. What can we sew for you?' I knew it was you." That was a relief for Barb. She asked Laurel if she'd found anything that could work for Madame Angelika's costume jacket.

"Yes, I did. It's the exact green I was looking for. Excellent find even if you had to go way down there into the creepy darkness." She held the velvet dress up to her work light for further inspection. "It's in great shape, too. And boy, did someone have a figure," she said as she held it up to her own frame before the wall of mirrors. "I know we'll be refashioning it for the svelte and striking Madame Angelika. But this is so well made, and the woman who wore it was obviously slender, too. We may be able to use some of the original sewing for the jacket."

As she inspected it more closely under the light, Laurel discovered the lining and the two embroidered sayings. "You're not going to believe what I just found in lining of this dress, Barb!"

"Save it for me. I'll be there soon. Looks like snow today, Laurel," she said as she tightened her muffler around her neck and stepped onto her bus.

Laurel let her fingers trace the writing in the lining. She couldn't believe what she was holding. "It's history! That's what this is. It's a piece of history in fabric form." That one word reminded Laurel that she hadn't finished rehearsing the sonnet for her 4 pm audition. There'd be no time for it once Barb arrived. She put the dress down and positioned her work light to create a pool of light on the floor. Grabbing the book of Shakespearean sonnets from the work shelf of costume books, she began:

Shall I compare thee to a summer's day?
Thou are lovelier and more temperate:
Rough winds do shake the darling buds of May,
And summer's lease hath all too short a date:
Sometime too hot the eye of heaven shines,
And often is his gold complexion dimm'd;

And every fair from fair sometime declines,
By chance, or nature's changing course, untrimm'd;
But thy eternal summer shall not fade
Nor lose possession of thou fair ow'st;
Nor shall Death brag thou wander'st in his shade,
When in eternal lines to time thou grow'st;
So long as men can breathe or eyes can see,
So long lives this, and this gives life to thee.

Laurel graciously bowed to her imaginary audience and added, "William Shakespeare, Sonnet 18." She continued with a New York accent and sarcasm, attempting to imitate an imagined casting director, "Thank you for your time, Ms. Edwards. We'll call you, should we have any questions. Oh, and we hope to cast the show before the end of December."

Just then the door opened and in came a bundled-up Barbara Morgenstern, Rand Theater's lead costume mistress of more than 20 years. She was a phenomenal seamstress with an eye for color, history, and period details. She could be sewing anywhere in the United States, but Chicago was home. She was a great mom and a very fun grandma: the rare kind of widow who spent the proper amount of time grieving and wallowing in the sadness that follows the death of one's husband. That had changed when her daughter's broken marriage brought her and her toddler twin boys back to Chicago. Barb opened her home and her heart, giving her daughter and her boys the master bedroom and her car. She insisted that she could deal with the city's train and bus system better than most people, and certainly better than a mom and her twin boys.

Laurel helped Barb take off her coat, unwound the muffler from around her neck, and deposited them onto the coat rack. "It's cold out there today and it smells like snow. Just feel my cheeks, Laurel."

"No thanks, and please don't say 'snow.' I have an audition at 4 o'clock today."

"How did your last one go?" Barb already knew the answer but needed to hear Laurel's dramatic retelling of how it went. It always involved a story.

Imitating the director's affected, snooty voice she said, "'We are looking for someone a little more mature.' For crying out loud, Barb, I'm in my 40s! The part is for someone in their 50s."

As she eyed Laurel's bohemian winter attire topped by a work apron filled with every pin ever made, Barb asked, "What were you wearing that day?" Laurel was like a graffitied alley wall.

"My below-the-knee brown tweed skirt, a cream colored high-neck silk blouse, my grandmother's cameo, and close-toed shoes. Not my boots."

"That sounds like a mature woman's outfit to me."

"Evidently not mature enough."

Barb changed into her work smock with one neatly placed Christmas pin that said, "Jesus is the Reason for the Season." She began gathering up things for her fitting with the lead male dancer for the Christmas show. Laurel took her seam ripper and started picking at the lining of the green velvet dress. "You've got to see this before I take it apart, Barb."

Barb walked over to the work table to look at the dress and to fill her apron pockets with some much-needed sewing tools. "Okay, what have we got here? What did you find in the lining of the dress?" she asked as she wound gold braiding onto a plastic board.

Isn't that something? It's two embroidered sayings by two different women: *Emma, Christmas Day 1880. Worn on the day when sorrow was no more,* and *Made by Rachel for Christmas in July 1945. Grateful to be grateful.* Shouldn't we turn this in to the Smithsonian or a historical society, instead of making a costume?" Laurel was absolutely serious.

"No, Laurel," argued Barb. "We should both get to work. You need to start the jacket for Madame Angelika and I need to finish my costume for her partner Vlad." Barb did voice the possible concern that Madame Angelika might have if she knew the costume she wore was made from 100-year old material. This thought immediately launched Laurel into another dramatic moment.

She pointed her toes in tendu and in a thick Russian accent she said, "Vhat two women made this costume from old clothes for the most important night of my life in America? Bring them to me!"

Laughing now, Barb directed Laurel to keep working on the dress as neither of them could afford to get fired weeks before Christmas. Laurel knew she was likely overreacting about an old piece of velvet, but she couldn't let go of the fact that she was holding history in her hands. She couldn't just ignore the sayings in the lining of this dress. Barb reminded her of how often they reused things, like the drapes from a castle that had been used for the soldiers' uniforms, and she held up Vlad's uniform. She mentioned all the netting and tulle from a rich donor's wedding that had been reused for tutus and dance skirts. "Rework, reuse, resew—that's been our personal long-time motto as seamstresses for the Rand's costuming department and it has saved the theater quite a bit of money." Barb lugged everything she needed for the fitting to the door.

Laurel pumped out two small cups of coffee from the hot pot. She handed one to Barb. Although she had a costume fitting appointment, she still had a few moments for this sweet ritual of their morning cup of coffee. "You're right, Barb. Okay, I'm changing subjects. How are your daughter and grandsons?"

Barb shared that Megan had gotten the job she had interviewed for and that the twins now called her "Nanny-Granny-Barb." She said that the twins were quite a handful if they didn't get to the park every day. "Lots of energy those two! Really, I couldn't be happier, Laurel. Children are a gift from God. I love it. And they are so excited about Christmas. How are you? I know you really wanted that part of Mrs. Banks in *Barefoot in The Park*."

"I did, but I am okay. I'll live. I always do," she said resignedly. "I haven't had a role in a very long time. To be honest, I was thinking it might be time to quit going for all these auditions."

"Nonsense! You seem alive when you audition, Laurel. It gives you hope." Barb decided to probe further about her personal life. "Are you headed home for Christmas this year?"

Laurel couldn't afford to go home and her family couldn't afford to come to her this year. Christmas would just be her and her cat. "Then you're coming to my house this Christmas, Laurel."

"Oh, Barb, I don't know. I don't want to be a fifth wheel."

Barb ignored that and began to describe a Morgenstern Christmas, telling Laurel she should arrive about 8 o'clock for an early breakfast on Christmas Eve. Barb went on to describe the rest of the day: ice skating, baking cookies, watching old Christmas classics while wrapping presents, and helping her make her famous red and green lasagna.

Interrupting Barb she asked, "Will you finally give me that recipe?!"

They would play games with the twins, deliver the cookies they'd made to the neighbors, eat lasagna, and head to church for midnight mass. She added that Laurel would need several changes of clothes and her pajamas as she would be spending the night, heading to bed only after she had helped Barb fill all of the stockings with care. "And Auntie Laurel, with two little boys you will need to sleep fast because you'll be waking up early on Christmas Day!"

By now, Laurel was wiping away tears. "Wow, how do I turn all of that down?"

"You can't. And I will not take no for an answer." Barb meant it. "You are not going to sit home alone on Christmas Eve and Christmas Day with your cat. Chester won't even miss you."

Laurel stared off into space, smoothing the remains of the green velvet dress over her lap. Her family went to midnight mass. She remembered the quiet reverence that filled the church, the angelic choir, the candlelit sanctuary. "I always wore a new dress on Christmas Eve," she mused. "I don't know why we — why I stopped going to church on Christmas Eve."

She folded the green velvet dress in half and smoothed out the lines that had been made in the velvet. She was embarrassed for sharing so much. She hated getting emotional. She felt out of control when it happened: Barb knew that about her and never made her feel bad about it. She was caught among three Christmases—in 1880, 1945, and a upcoming one in 1992. "Oh Barb, there's just something about this dress and its lining." Standing up now, she announced her decision: "I'm going to save the lining and sew it into the costume for Madame Angelika!"

Barb put her coffee mug away. "Great. Madame Angelika will have your head on a Christmas platter, or rather both of our heads."

"Two women sewed their lives into this velvet. I'll place it in an inconspicuous spot on the back panel of her jacket or in a sleeve. She won't know it's there, but I will."

"Then why don't you embroider something into the lining?"

This was not a dare. She was asking Laurel to go a little deeper instead of playing it safe all the time. Just as coming to her family's Christmas celebration would be a risk for her, personalizing the lining, would be, well, personal. Laurel met up with Barb at the door. "I just might do that, Barbara Morgenstern."

As she exited through the door, Barb added, "Include your name and the year, Laurel. Just like the others did."

Laurel returned to the smart green evening dress and held it up to the front of her own body. She looked into the long wall mirror, trying to imagine the woman who wore this dress. "What an awesome lady you were Rachel from 1945. And you, too, Emma from 1880." Sitting down at the work table, she grabbed a spiral notepad and pen. "Okay, Laurel, what will you embroider? Something true and lasting. Something wise from your vast experience in the arts. Who knows? Years from now someone might read this." Laurel took a few moments, and then she penned the words to be embroidered into the lining of the green velvet: *Sewn by Laurel for a prima ballerina, Christmas 1992. Dance when there is no audience to applaud you.*

Laurel gracefully executed a short dance to music that only she heard. As the last notes faded, she bowed deeply. Coming up from her bow she whispered, *Dance when there is no audience to applaud you, Laurel Edwards.*

Sewn by Laurel for a Prima
Ballerina. Christmas 1992.
Dance when there is no
audience to applaud you

Madame Angelika called Laurel and Barb to her dressing room several days after the show opened. She wanted to know, "Is it an American custom to sew sayings into the linings of costumes?"

Laurel answered that yes, America women sometimes embroidered into clothing and other things of sentimental value. She speculated that the original green velvet dress must have had a story and said that she just couldn't toss the lining away. Laurel apologized and offered to remake the costume if that's what she wanted. "The third saying was mine. I meant it only as an encouragement to you, Madame Angelika. It brought great encouragement to me as I embroidered it for you."

Angelika said, through tears and great emotion, "You will do no such thing with my costume! Every night before I step onto the stage I dance in front of my dressing mirror in this jacket. I dance to honor the King of Kings who gave me life, made my limbs, and gave me the gift of dance. It is my prayer to hear His applause first before the audience's kind applause. His means more to me. May I keep the costume? I want to take it back to Russia and show it to my dance instructor and my family."

Barb and Laurel were stunned. They'd never been called to a dressing room to be thanked for making a costume, nor had anyone asked to keep a dance costume. They were usually in bad shape by the end of a show. Barb spoke up first. "We are honored that you would want to keep the costume, Madame Angelika. Can we check back with you about keeping it?"

"Of course. Thank you, Ms. Barb and Ms. Laurel. Merry Christmas to both of you!" And she graciously bowed in thanks.

Laurel and Barb floated back to the sewing workroom stunned by this moment with a prima ballerina in her dressing room. Laurel was so glad that she had embroidered those words.

Barb poured Laurel a cup of coffee and asked her if she was going to be having a Morgenstern Christmas or a Chester-the-Cat Christmas? Clinking her coffee mug against Barb's she said, "I'll spend it with you as long as I can bring presents and something for everyone's stocking."

Barb was thrilled and said they would welcome the kindness of being remembered by Auntie Laurel. Thus began a tradition of Laurel Edwards and Barbara Morgenstern spending every Christmas Eve and Christmas Day together, no matter what was going on in their lives. And yes, Laurel got the recipe for Barb's red and green lasagna and became the maker of a big pan of it every Christmas Eve. The secret to this recipe was all about the homemade spaghetti and pesto sauces. "Don't use the jar kind," Laurel told everyone. "It just isn't the same lasagna."

❧ JULIE ❧

J ulie walked into her office and sewing room holding a Moses basket that held the most precious thing she had ever carried. It was her six-week old son. Weeks before, the basket had been filled with baby gifts from the staff and families of her department at the college. She looked like Mary, the mother of Jesus, with a blue fuzzy blanket draped over her head. She steadied herself as she made her way across the dimly lit room. She had become adept at carrying her child and other things all at the same time. She sometimes hummed a circus tune quietly imagining herself as a tightrope walker. "That's right, Julie, keep your humor or you'll burst into tears for lack of sleep."

She immediately noticed the coldness of the room and was glad she had the extra blanket. She took it off of her head and tucked it around her son's little body. She tightened her robe, pulled the collar up, and closed it around her neck. "Hello, office!" she said with a smile, "I haven't seen you in a while." It was truly a place of sanctuary and Julie hadn't been in it for almost two months. It held two sewing machines, shelves and shelves of fabrics, a colorful display of spools of thread, dozens of scissors, and various sewing notions organized in eclectic oversized glass containers. Her personal and professional library filled the shelves with books, textbooks, notebooks, and magazines that were all neatly organized with color and pizzazz.

"All right, my sweet boy. Your mommy, a former designer and college professor, needs to get moving on a Sunshine Quilt for a woman who needs some hope today."

Julie moved her son to the chair and ottoman where she used to sit for hours. She had read that talking to babies helped with brain and language development. She talked to her son every day about everything. She'd spell things, explain things, describe things, sing things, all in simple but informative ways.

"The word for the day is 'hope.' I will spell it for you. H-O-P-E. You can't taste it or touch it. Sometimes you can see it in someone's eyes or their smile. But most of the time hope is something you feel and know deep inside your mind and heart." She touched her son's head and chest on the words "mind" and "heart."

A draft from the old windows and the chill of October hit Julie, sending a shiver through her whole body. She had forgotten how cold it got in this part of the house in the fall. She took a small quilt off of a pile of stacked quilts and placed it on top of the baby basket, making a little tent of warmth for her son. She found some mail on her desk. Julie opened up a package from a friend and pulled out a green velvet jacket and a card. It read:

Dear Julie,

Congratulations on the birth of your son, Jeremy! Here is a gift card to your favorite restaurant for you and Tomas. Go there soon. You two deserve it! And here is a very unusual piece of real velvet. I know how you love fabrics that have some kind of ancient value. I found it at an estate sale and it screamed 'Julie,' so I bought it for you. It was inside a smashed white gift box tied up with a red satin bow. Sounds like a fabric story, right? I want to know all about it when I come to visit you and your precious son.

Love always, Sami

Julie turned to her son, "My good friend's name is Sami. Her name is actually Samantha. We went to college together." She brushed his cheek with the sleeve of the jacket and said, "Soft." Julie then began rattling off information about velvet like she was in a lecture hall standing before a group of students: "Velvet is a soft pile fabric that's been manufactured for almost 4,000 years. It's a luxury fabric. Velvet can be made from any type of thread, but silk thread is costlier and more beautiful than cotton."

She held the jacket up and smoothed it across her robe to look at herself in the full length mirror on the wall. "What is this?" she said trying to make the material appear longer. "It's a costume for a very slender woman, and what a nice shade of green." She inspected it further and found the hand embroidered words in the lining. She then turned the jacket inside out reveal the rest of them. "Three people have embroidered words into this lining!"

Emma, Christmas Day 1880.
Worn on the day when sorrow was no more.

Made by Rachel for Christmas in July 1945.
Grateful to be grateful.

Sewn by Laurel for a prima ballerina, Christmas 1992.
Dance when there is no audience to applaud you.

Julie's eyes were filled with tears. "Darn hormones! Oh, Lord, what am I holding in my hands?" She realized she was holding more than a velvet costume. She was holding history. She reasoned that the costume couldn't have been worn by someone in 1880 or 1945. No, someone had reused the velvet and saved the lining. "It must have been a dress that a woman made and wore in 1880. They used yards and yards of material back then." She let her fingers trace the old embroidered words as she said them out loud, "*Worn on the day when sorrow was no more.* Oh my, she must have experienced a huge loss." Her fingers traced over the next one: "*Made by Rachel for Christmas in July of 1945. Grateful to be grateful.* World War II ended around 1945." She then imagined the material from the 1880 dress refashioned into another dress. "Maybe a woman celebrating the return of her husband from the war and wearing a green velvet dress in July? Phew, that would be a hot number in more ways than one!"

Julie realized her voice was getting louder with each guess. Whispering now, she continued tracing the embroidery with her finger, "And this little velvet number was made for a dancer: a prima ballerina in 1992." Just then Julie heard a familiar voice. It was Maggie, her assistant.

Maggie, a brilliant graduate student and Julie's assistant, waltzed into the room looking absolutely put together and fabulous. She hugged Julie, reminding her that it had been weeks since they'd been together. She then admired her flannel pajamas and robe, joking that she always looked good in plaid. Embarrassed Julie said, "I know, I know, Maggie. I haven't showered either. I just can't get my days and nights to work out with this little one, so I wear flannel most days."

Maggie turned all of her attention to the baby. Julie shared how wonderful it was to be a parent even though she was tired. She said it was one of the best things that had ever happened to her and Tomas. "I don't remember what I was doing before he was born."

She interrupted Julie with laughter saying, "Of course, you remember, Julie! You were working at the Art Institute."

"Ugh, which reminds me that I don't have the class syllabus done yet." Maggie told her she had another week before it was due. Then she announced that she was giving Julie a whole day and evening to herself. She had worked it out with Tomas. She had bottles, clothes, blankets, and everything else Jeremy would need.

Maggie told her, "You can work on the class syllabus (but I wouldn't). You can do whatever you'd like to do today, or you can do nothing. Take a long nap. Watch a movie. Go shopping. It's your day!"

Now Julie was interrupting Maggie with laughter and disbelief. "Really? My husband and you planned this day for me?!"

Maggie picked up Jeremy and the basket. "I'm sorry but we need to be on our way. And you know I was a nanny, so I can do this." Then Maggie noticed that Julie had grabbed her sketch pad and several colored pencils. "What are you working on in this cold, drafty room?"

She held up the costume piece. "I'm working with history! This is about a yard of green velvet history and hope."

Maggie started for the door. "Well, it looks like you know what you want to do. We are going to leave now, Mommy."

Julie dashed across the room and took one last peek at her son. "Goodbye, my little one. Have fun with your Auntie Maggie." That personal description caused Maggie to tear up. It would be a long time before she would ever be an 'Aunt Maggie.' But this was the way Julie was about everyone in her life. No one was a stranger. Every person was of ultimate value and importance. Everyone one was included, everyone was family.

Julie hugged Maggie. "Thank you. It means so much that you would do this for me." Julie scooped up the pink bakery box that Maggie had brought her. "And this means a great deal to me, too."

Julie sat down in her favorite chair and opened the file for the Sunshine Quilt recipient. She began to read it aloud:

PATIENT'S NAME: Marla Bradshaw.

My sophomore college roommate was named Marla. Marla Baker.

RESIDENCE: Whispering Hope Rehabilitation Center.

I like the name of her facility.

REASON FOR REHABILITATION & THERAPY: Multiple injuries sustained from an automobile accident. Limited mobility. Wheelchair bound. Occupational and physical therapy is needed for full rehabilitation and ambulation.

Marla, you're alive and you're a miracle!

MARITAL STATUS: Widow. Mrs. Bradshaw's husband was a fatality in the automobile crash.

Oh, Marla… I'm so sorry.

PROGNOSIS, EMOTIONAL AND PHYSICAL: The rehabilitation plan is for complete recovery and ambulation but progress has slowed to do patient's depression.

Oh, dear Marla.

SPIRITUAL STATUS: Religious.

I hope no one ever describes me as religious.

COMMENTS: A lap quilt for Mrs. Bradshaw would be meaningful and might raise her interest in rehabilitation once again.

FAVORITE COLORS: Jewel tones such as red, blue, purple, gold, and green.

She loves green!

"Mrs. Marla Bradshaw, you shall have your quilt and it will have green in it," said Julie hugging the costume jacket and the file. She opened a sketch pad and began to draw out a quilt design. She measured the lining pieces that held the embroidered sayings from years long ago. She had already decided she was going to include her own embroidered sentiment for the quilt, right alongside the other ones.

Julie decided that she would use most of the remaining velvet for the quilt. Knowing Mrs. Bradshaw loved jewel tones made the choice of colors easy. She would make sure the batting would be warm but not too heavy on Mrs. Bradshaw's legs.

She decided that she would research velvet bought and sold in the United States during the late 1800s and hunt for photographs of spouses welcoming soldiers home during World War II. She would also follow-up with Sami about where she had purchased the costume. The rhinestone snowflake button hinted that it had been a winter show. Samantha's present residence was in Illinois, which narrowed down the theater to somewhere around Chicago.

It was already mid-October. Thanksgiving would be the perfect time to deliver it, but it seemed unlikely she could finish it while caring for her new baby. If she got to work on it today, it would be several weeks, even a month. Then she remembered a couple of textiles students who needed projects for the close of the semester in January. Maybe they could help her with some of the quilt's work.

Julie stood up and firmly pronounced: "Marla Bradshaw, I am going to tell you all I can find out about these three women so that you won't give up. Oh, please Lord, don't let her give up. Hold on to His hope, Marla." She was buoyed by this final thought that she would be sewing hope into Marla Bradshaw's quilt. She'd sewn quilts for all kinds of reasons, but she had never been called upon to sew one of such consequence or importance.

Julie hurried downstairs and made herself a good strong cup of coffee. She ate the delicious chocolate chip pumpkin muffin that Maggie had brought to her, savoring every bite. Next, she'd shower, change into something more interesting than flannel pajamas, and go shopping for fabric that would complement the velvet.

"Lord, I have my work cut out for me!" She laughed at her own silly pun. That was the kind of joke her husband was great at making. That reminded her that it had been days, maybe a week, since her husband had eaten a home-cooked meal. They'd been eating the wonderful meals people prepare for families with a new baby, but not one from their kitchen. Julie grabbed everything for chili and began browning a pound of ground beef. She chopped onions and garlic and loaded the crock pot with chili beans, whole plum tomatoes, tomato sauce, and spices. By the time she had showered and changed her clothes the house smelled delicious. Tomas would certainly wonder who came over and cooked a meal for them in the crockpot, as it seemed unlikely that she would have done this!

It took more than several weeks to complete the quilt for Marla Bradshaw. A couple of her students helped with the details of the quilt. Some of them had never quilted before so it was a great learning experience that prompted them to try their hand at quilted potholders for Christmas gifts. She encouraged them further over coffee, suggesting that potholders would seem easy compared to what they were about to mail to Marla Bradshaw. "Thank you so much! I truly couldn't have done it without your help."

Julie finished the letter to Marla that she would tuck it inside the box with the quilt. If UPS—the United Problem Solvers—was as good as its word, Marla would receive her quilt a few weeks before Christmas. Julie wanted her to be able to show it to her family and friends.

The lengthy letter told Marla all that she had learned from her investigation into the green velvet. She wrote that she believed every woman must have led a life of hope, holding onto its tangible intangibleness. She shared that she believed God took care of each one of them. She also said she was praying that this very same hope would lay over Marla's legs with the lap quilt and that she would regain her ability to walk. She had chosen Romans 5 for her embroidered words sewn alongside the other women's words: *And this hope does not lead to disappointment.*

She also included all that she had learned from her conversations, by letter, with prima ballerina Angelika Belov. She told her how much Ms. Belov wanted to keep the jacket as a remembrance of her dance work in America, but that she returned it to the costume mistresses as a gift. She also shared how heartbroken Barb and Laurel were when the costume was separated from them when their department moved to a new location. She told her how overjoyed she was to find out Julie's friend had bought it at an estate sale of a collector of theater costumes. She also shared about her phone conversations with Madame Angelika Belov. She wrote, "Marla, I just had to hear her delightful Russian voice that Barb and Laurel had spoken about, and that Laurel could imitate. I wanted to also hear the depth of emotion that filled every correspondence that she exchanged with me."

During one phone call Angelika told Julie that she danced every night for the woman who knew the great sorrow, and for the woman whose husband had been in the war, and for her costume mistress, Laurel, whose embroidered words inspired her to dance more with her heart and not just her legs, feet, and arms. She wrote that Angelika said, "Every night my legs moved for these women. Please tell Mrs. Bradshaw that her legs will move again. I will ask God to heal them."

Julie told her that visiting with Laurel and Barb was like talking to two favorite relatives. The conversations were long and filled with hilarious, memorable, and startling stories. Generous and kind Barb had even sent baby clothes to Julie from her two grandsons. They were grateful that their costume jacket had come into the possession of such a skilled young textiles professor. They had never made a costume from a dated piece of clothing with such an unusual history—and they had never become so close to a lead in one of the shows at the Rand Theater.

Julie believed she had located Rachel's family, the Ryders. She had not heard back from them yet. She was hopeful that they would respond, as none of her correspondence had been returned by mail. She was still researching velvet made in the U.S. during the late 1800s. She was certain she would be able to fill in some details of Emma's history at a later date, as well as Rachel Ryder's. "This will give me another reason to contact you, Marla. I hope you will feel the same way I do about connecting, as I would love to know what happens with your quilt."

It's amazing what can be crafted with tiny scraps of material and Julie was an expert at these kinds of things. Nothing went to waste in her workroom. Julie combined a piece of the remaining green velvet with other scraps of the fabrics she had used in the quilt and fashioned them into three small art pieces resembling the likeness of Marla's quilt. One went to Madame Angelika Belov in Russia. One was for Laurel and Barb, who planned to hang it in their sewing workroom to remind them that costume work truly matters. The third one would be mailed to Rachel Ryder's family once they were located.

She was certain the story was going to come full circle, because that's what God did so often in her own story. Just as Marla's quilt was finally complete, so would the story of the green velvet Christmas dress come full circle.

The last thing Julie made with the remaining scrap of the green velvet was a silhouette of what she imagined was Emma's 1800's green velvet

Christmas dress. At the bottom of the art she penned all of the embroidered sayings, never wanting to forget a single word or year. She then had her two students sign their names to her art piece, and she signed her own name and the year. The finished art was hung on the wall the day after Marla Bradshaw's lap quilt was mailed to commemorate its finish and their handiwork. The group decided to properly toast and celebrate its completion with pumpkin chocolate chip muffins and coffee, of course.

Quilt made by Marla Bradshaw. Christmas 2007. "and this Hope does not lead to disappointment." Romans 5

T hat day, Marla decided to get up instead of staying in bed. She got dressed with the help of Yuko, her occupational therapist. She did her morning physical therapy much to the surprise of two physical therapists who hadn't seen her in more than a week. The therapy hurt just as it had hurt for a long time.'

She ate lunch at a table in the dining room rather than going back to her room as was her habit. Instead of a chair, Marla sat in the wheelchair that seemed to confine and define her. Lunch was tomato soup and tuna melts. It was a cold and rainy day and the soup was soothing. Marla felt tired and decided to cut her conversation short with the kind gentleman who remained at her table. "Mr. Smithers, please excuse me. I am feeling a bit tired and need to go rest before my next therapy."

On the way back to her room, one of the nurses told her that a package had come for her. She said it was likely the Bible study materials from her church. Someone mailed them to her, as she didn't want anyone bringing them to the hospital. The nurse assured her that this package was larger than Bible study materials.

Waiting on her bedside table was a box wrapped in brown mailing paper. She didn't recognize the name or address of the sender, a Julie Bayer. On the back of the box two handprints had been traced. One was adult-sized hand and the other was undeniably a tiny baby's hand. Underneath the handprints were the neatly printed words, "We prayed for you today, Marla." Her eyes filled with tears at the thought of such a kind gesture from a complete stranger. Just then her favorite nurse came into her room. Jim always had a joke of the day following lunch, and this time he had a pair of scissors, too. For more than a week his jokes had not brought one bit of cheer to her heart. Yet Nurse Jim didn't give up on telling them to her.

"I thought you might need some help with your package," and he handed her a pair of scissors.

"Jim, how do you do that?"

"Do what?" he asked as he freshened her water.

"Anticipate the needs of your patients."

"When you've been doing this job for as long as I have, you learn to ask yourself, 'What would I need if I was Marla?' That's all it is. Anyone can do that."

Marla's hands were shaking. Seeing this, Jim took the scissors from her, snipped a corner of the paper, and handed them back to her. He told her that he'd be back later with a cup of afternoon tea. She cut through the brown paper and opened the box. On top of the neatly folded tissue paper was the letter from Julie. The letter explained the Sunshine Quilt Foundation and that the social worker at the rehab center had filled out a form that generated the making of this lap quilt. Julie went on to explain how she had made the quilt to encourage Marla's story in rehabilitating after such a huge loss. She shared the stories she had discovered about the green velvet costume jacket with its lining filled with embroidered sentiments. She also explained why she had chosen the Romans 5 scripture and stitched it alongside the other phrases chosen by the previous owners of the velvet. She wrote, "Yours is about hope, Marla." It read: *"Quilt made by Julie for Marla Bradshaw, Christmas 2007. "… and this Hope does not lead to disappointment. Romans 5."*

Marla unwrapped layers and layers of green and red tissue from around the quilt. She smoothed the quilt out on top of her bed and began admiring Julie's handiwork. She turned it over and with one of her fingers she began to trace the quotes of the women of the green velvet Christmas dress. The old fabric was still so soft and plush. She held it to her cheek and felt the goodness in the green velvet. She then began to cry a little, which turned into weeping that required several tissues. She was humbled that someone would take the time to make something so beautiful and meaningful for someone they didn't even know. A day earlier she had considered returning to her home and hiring a home health nurse to help her live out the rest of her life. But in the short span of a few minutes with this gift, that became a distant thought. She felt a flurry of other emotions stirring inside of her.

She wanted to call Julie and thank her for the quilt. She wanted to ring her buzzer for Nurse Jim and show the quilt to him, too. But most important, she needed to contact the director of rehab to set up an appointment to discuss future goals for learning how to walk again. So many thoughts surged through her body, heart, mind, soul, and spirit. One very important emotion was rising inside of her: hope. She hadn't felt it since before her husband's passing.

Marla pushed her room buzzer. Soon Jim appeared and she held up the quilt for him. "I just received the most incredible gift, Jim! Just look at this! It's a handmade lap quilt from a complete stranger. Isn't it beautiful?"

He came over to examine it. "Yes, this is very beautiful, Marla!" He then shared about his wife's quilt work and asked if he could take a picture of it to show to her.

Marla said, "Of course you can. But first, could you take one of me and the quilt for my quiltmaker, Julie? She gave me her cell number as she wanted to know when I received it." Jim took her cell phone and readied it for a photo as Marla smoothed the quilt out and held up the ends close her face. She was smiling a big smile—a smile Jim had never seen on Marla Bradshaw's face. He retold one of his funny jokes about her racing down the hall in a walker someday and a huge guffaw and smile crossed her face again.

It was a perfect photo of Marla and the quilt. She stared at her toothy grinning face and felt a flush of embarrassment rush to her cheeks. But Marla didn't care and joked about how hot it felt in her room at that moment. Jim assured her that the temperature hadn't changed, and that perhaps it was the excitement of the last few minutes. He asked if she'd like a cranberry special but she asked instead if Jim could see if Holly, the director of rehabilitation therapy, would meet with her or set up an appointment for tomorrow. She needed to discuss her future goals for rehabilitating and walking. Such joy flooded her heart. It was the hope that she had prayed for on the loneliest of nights.

Every day her physical and occupational therapies pushed her to new levels. Learning to walk again was no easy task. The brain and the body had to decide to work together, and it took time to heal. Patience with herself was the key for Marla: healing simply took time.

Suddenly Marla welcomed visits with friends and family to talk about her wonderful quilt and about Jesus's love for them. Some of her friends reported their concern to the nurse's station about how she seemed emotional, wound up, and overly talkative. Others listened intently and asked questions. Marla loved to answer the questions about the quilt and her new desire to walk again.

As the days drew closer to Christmas, the story of the quilt and the green velvet sewn into it became even better. Julie filled in more of the historical and relational details that she had gathered, and Marla padded them, just a little bit. She had been a high school English teacher and they are, often, great writers. One interested patient, Mrs. Novikoff, didn't mind her new visitor, Mrs. Bradshaw. They were very formal about their names with one another. It had started when their shared rehab therapists referred to them with these titles and it just continued with the way they spoke to each other. Marla had observed Mrs. Novikoff had only a few visitors, and as time went by they naturally fell into sharing far beyond the PT Room, at meals, and eventually in each other's rooms. One day, Mrs. Novikoff bravely shared the story of how she had lost her leg to the effects of diabetes. Marla then shared about the car crash that took her husband's life, severely injured both of her legs, and left her feeling hopeless about ever walking again.

"As I told you yesterday, Mrs. Novikoff, loneliness and depression had set up camp down the hall in room 212. I was disappointed and defeated by my story. Losing my ability to walk was one thing, but losing my husband was so very painful. I didn't want to go on anymore. I was ready to give up and go home in a wheelchair. Then this gift arrived—this colorful lap quilt changed it all for me. Would you like to hold it?"

Mrs. Novikoff loved Marla's quilt and often admired it. She loved the design, but even more she loved the feel of the velvet and satin against her legs. She looked at Laurel's words once again. She had looked at all of them on her last visit with Marla. "So soft," she murmured as she spread the quilt over her legs.

Marla picked up Julie's most recent letter and shared a couple of things about Rachel, Laurel, Barb, Julie, and their embroidered words. Mrs. Novikoff admired the beauty of the quilt as she shared their stories. She had never fully mastered the English language but she understood everything. "I like these women of the quilt. Share more with me." That was all Marla needed to hear. The story was winding down, and she felt certain that it was time to share about Christ's birth.

"And that's what Jesus' birth at Christmas is all about. This one incredible gift sent more than 2,000 years ago expressly to you, Mrs.

Novikoff, and to me. God's costly extravagant love in the form of his Son. I'm going to get a little preachy here, if you'll allow me. Would that be all right with you?" Mrs. Novikoff nodded yes to Marla.

"The Word of God tells us that Christ came when we were utterly helpless, at just the right time, and died for us. Most people would not be willing to die for an upright person, though someone might, perhaps, be willing to die for a person who is especially good. But God showed his great love for us by sending Christ to die for us while we were still sinners. Can you imagine such a gift?"

Mrs. Novikoff shook her head no. She could not imagine that kind of a gift for her. She had done nothing with her life to deserve this kind of a gift from God. Marla understood. How she had wept on the day she received the quilt from Julie! She, too, felt she didn't deserve such a magnificent gift from a stranger who barely knew her. But the gift changed her life and gave her the desire to hope again.

"I turned to Jesus and asked Him to help me live a better story than the one I had been living."

Marla felt the time had come in their relationship to see if Mrs. Novikoff would like to know the hope and love she had found in knowing Jesus. She shook her head yes this time, folded her hands, and bowed her head. Marla then laid her hands on Mrs. Novikoff's shoulder and prayed for her to receive Jesus into her heart. Mrs. Novikoff's face looked so different after she prayed with Marla. Tears glistened on her cheeks and she looked like a burden had been lifted off of her.

"My heart feels very different now," she said. "My family came from the same part of Russia as Madame Belov. I learned how to dance as a child just like she did. I like the story of the green velvet ballerina jacket and the costume ladies best of all." There was a pause as Mrs. Novikoff lifted the quilt off her leg and drew up her pant leg to reveal the prosthetic attached to her knee. "I do not think I will ever dance again."

"I don't think I will either." Marla took the other woman's hands in hers. "But we will both learn to walk again, won't we?" They smiled at one another, knowing this was their future story, together.

Marla became penpals with Laurel and Barb, who still worked at the Rand Theater. In a recent letter they promised to visit Marla and Julie. Barb added, "And we need to do it before Laurel is old-er and gray-er." To which Laurel had mocked in her paragraph, "And before Barb gets her second set of knees!"

Through Julie's careful research with Laurel's and Barb's help, Rachel Ryder's family had finally been located. Her granddaughter, Jennifer, received the green velvet artwork Julie made. She proudly displayed it next to a photo of Grandma Ray-Ray in her green velvet dress. Marla's picture of her holding the lap quilt completed the Ryder's collection. It remains one of the family's favorite stories to tell.

Full circle. It was just as Julie had hoped and prayed it would turn out. The story of the green velvet Christmas dress had come full circle.

Marla knew that the friendly repartee she shared with Jim masked the change that was coming soon. Discussion was underway regarding her release back home. She felt both uneasy and excited about returning there. The Thursday GriefShare meetings held at Whispering Hope Rehab had been helpful and supportive of her story. She planned to continue going to them. She felt more and more confident about life without her husband, but the ache of his absence remained. Her faithful lab, Hannah, would now be her constant companion. At least someone she knew and loved would be there to welcome her home.

Whispering Hope Rehab Center had been the right place for her recovery. Marla could walk down the hallway with a walker now. She no longer needed the wheelchair. The next challenge was a four-pronged cane. She had tried it, but it was hard to let go of the comfort and safety of the walker. She could see why they attached seats to them but she asked rehab to order one without a seat for her as she didn't plan to have it for long.

This was the new Marla Bradshaw making headway in her healing process. The rehab therapists loved bragging about her accomplishments in the weekly PT progress reports. She actually was a great encourager to other patients. The staff often sent Marla to visit a particularly discouraged patient. She always found a way in their door of despair or frustration. Her secret weapon was wise and very simple: she would tell her story, then ask them a question to draw out their story. She cautioned others against interrupting people when they were sharing their story, and to not make one life story seem more important than another. Marla knew that listening involved the ears and eyes, so she often visited without her phone to reduce distractions. She became known as "Marla Bradshaw, Whispering Hope's Therapist-at-Large." They wanted to get her a name badge with that inscription but she declined, knowing she wasn't planning to live there much longer.

As the days drew close for Marla's discharge, she decided to use her remaining two occupational therapy sessions making cupcakes with Yuko. Making dozens of red velvet cupcakes was no small task with a walker but she managed with Yuko's help.

The day came for Marla's discharge. It was near Valentine's Day and the dining room was festive with the usual holiday decorations. During her graduation celebration from rehab people shared Marla Bradshaw stories, ate cupcakes, and drank tea. There were a few tears shed. One doesn't easily part company with one's rehab therapy staff and the nurses that have seen almost every part of you and taught you how to care for yourself and to walk once again. Not to mention the dear ones that have been with you through the pain, anger, frustration, disappointment, grieving and the loss of your hope and direction.

Finally, it was time to say goodbye. It was ironic for Marla to be wheeled out of the place where she had learned to walk, but hospital rules are hospital rules! Marla hugged Yuko one more time. They promised to remain friends beyond the rehab center's walls. Jim and his wife lived about 20 minutes from Marla's home. It was reassuring to know that. Jim wheeled Marla to the door of the rehab center and told her he'd be checking on her later that night. He pressed the automatic door button and as the huge double doors opened, he cheerfully warned her that she had better behave herself in the coming days.

The wheelchair came to a stop. Marla took a deep breath, stood up by herself, and grabbed the walker that Jim unfolded for her. She pivoted around to face him. She hugged and thanked this dear nurse for being the unforgettable, fun-loving, caring, and sometimes stern nurse that she had needed to recover and heal. She also confessed that she had had her doubts about having a male nurse, as all of her other nurses had been females. "But you cured me, Jim!" He began to laugh as he opened the car door. Marla had made the joke this time, and it was a good one, according to Jim. It felt good to leave Whispering Hope Rehab Center with laughter instead of tears.

Life began again for Marla Bradshaw. She wrote her book, *Conquering Hope*. To this day she travels about her own state, sometimes out of the country, to tell the story of how hope conquers all things, especially at Christmas time. She always brings her quilt with her when she tells the story. It tells the truth about the stories of the women and their embroidered sayings, sewn among the remaining green velvet on the backside of the quilt. She lets people hold the quilt so that they can enjoy the detail of Julie's work and trace their fingers across those words marked with time and relationships. She doesn't care if the embroidery or satin lining gets worn or smudged in the process. Each word of each line is being remembered in that moment, just as Emma had hoped that her words and the goodness in the green velvet would outlast her lifetime. And so, they did, dear Emma. And so, it did.

Love bears all things, believes all things, hopes all things, endures all things. Love never fails. And Hope stands up tall to hold hands with this kind of Love.

God's love and abiding hope helped Emma live her life after her husband and two children passed away. Hope came in two shapes that Christmas in 1880. One was a bolt of green velvet fabric from McGeevy's Mercantile. The other was a relationship with Jesus Christ—an extravagant gift—sent by God the Father, while she was in the darkness and despair of her own story. He came because Emma's story mattered to Him—just as your story matters to Him.

L oss of a life is never far away from our stories. We'd like it to be far, far away from it though, wouldn't we? Loss is always there in some form or another. It could be the loss of a relationship, a job, a dream, a ministry, a cherished item, a skill, or a physical ability. It's a certainty—there will be loss in our lives. The important question is, how will we deal with our losses? And what will be our living legacy?

The year I began writing the play, *The Green Velvet Christmas Dress*, my sister Melanee's husband, Ken, passed away. No one was prepared for his early entrance into the Lord's presence. It left my sister and her family in great pain. I watched her stunning grieving process along with her children's. I listened and prayed with her often. It was a privilege to walk so intimately in that kind of a story. I believe it was the doorway into writing the play and the eventual story of *The Green Velvet Christmas Dress*.

My sister's fourth daughter and my niece, Juliana, was the first to hear my faltering telling of a very short story version before it became the play. She was staying with us the summer after her father's passing while taking a missions course here in California. It meant a great deal to care for her. Juliana's approval of the story was a nod of "yes" from God to move forward in writing the play.

The play begins with Emma sharing the story of her deep loss and her hope for the dress's living legacy as she makes final embroidery stitches in the lining, "Oh my, how I've prayed for this dress. It's going to carry a message that will live on for years." In the book, as she makes the first cut into the velvet, she prays these purposeful words, "Father, if there truly is a goodness in the green velvet, then bring it forth as I cut out this dress and begin to make it."

The play had a successful two-year run, which spurred me on to expand the story in 2013. The beginning writing process of *The Green Velvet Christmas Dress* story was fraught with a great deal of emotion. I had to go back in time to tell Emma's story. I can quickly recall the pain and heartache that I felt as I wrote about the loss of her husband and two children. I wept through much of the writing of those words of such a deep loss with greater detail than the play had described. For weeks I could not write another word of the story and the plotline. I tried and tried. I am not one to force the writing of a story, but I had never had one so profoundly affect me to the point of deep loss and grief. I finally put the writing aside.

In an interesting parallel to Emma's story, I told myself I would return to the story someday. It was as if I neatly folded the green velvet and put the story away in a someday dresser drawer.

And remarkably, the goodness in the green velvet came and was unfolded in the midst of my own physical hardship. I had a stroke in the spring of 2015 (actually I had two). I was told I would never walk again. Although I felt certain of God's ability to heal me, nothing proved this in my physical story. My feet and legs were numb, and I could not move them. My speech was affected, which was very scary for me as a storyteller. My arms were weak and felt clumsy and awkward. My mind was fuzzy and narrowed with thoughts of my future as a mom, a wife, an artist—as Melea. All sorts of doubts about what would become of me were tangled up as I wondered *What will be my life story now—my living legacy?*

God was very real to me in my rehabilitation story. Daytime was busy with physical, occupational, and speech rehab therapy. My nurses and therapists were so very good to me. I got to know several wonderful chaplains at the hospital. Twice I was allowed to tell stories to other patients and their friends and family in the chapel as part of my speech therapy. But the nights were hard. The therapists would go home, and the nursing shifts would change about 7 p.m. My kind prayer visitors and my tired husband, David, would leave around 9 p.m. The doors were closed, the room lights were turned down, and the halls became quiet. Being alone was difficult unless a kind friend spent the night. What a gift they were to me as they coiled themselves up on a pull-out chair to sleep beside me. I fell asleep talking about everything and nothing with them. If there wasn't someone there with me, I had my trusty phone with its scripture and worship music to lull me to sleep.

I returned home in a wheelchair after more than five weeks in the hospital and rehab therapy. I wore an ankle-foot orthotic brace for my right leg and there was much more physical therapy ahead if I wanted to walk again. With an at-home therapist's help I moved from a wheelchair to a walker. Later I replaced the walker with a four-pronged cane and finally with a single-tipped cane. It would be another year before I walked without support.

Val and Vicki, two dear friends and sisters, did not leave me alone in my story. They had visited me in the hospital and after I returned home. On a warm summer evening after we had eaten dinner Vicki asked me, "Melea, what happened to *The Green Velvet Christmas Dress*?" (They both had been in the play and felt a certain kind of investment in the story and its writer.)

I knew where I had left Emma on the page. I grabbed my computer, searched for the story doc, and shared what I had written with Vicki, Val, and David. We all cried together over Emma's story. That night, after telling what I had written of *The Green Velvet Christmas Dress* (I was storytelling again!), we committed to meet one Saturday a month. Val and Vicki would come for dinner and I would read/storytell the next portion of the story. These dinners saved me, in many ways. (I was a writer once again!) The story kept me moving forward in my physical healing, too. I was accountable to three other people to finish the story, and to many others to learn to walk again.

The goodness in the green velvet was very real and no longer in a someday dresser drawer for me. I have come to realize that I was living my legacy in all of those moments—while in the hospital, after the hospital, and even before the hospital. I have learned that we are not meant to live our stories alone. We are meant to live them out loud and on purpose, with others, and with God leading the way.

Oh, I still limp from my stroke. I have balance and gait issues and sometimes trip over my words or confuse one word with another. My arms are not as strong as I hoped they'd be four years later. However, I would never trade the slower gait, the lack of balance, the less-than-perfect speech, nor the weakness in my arms for all that I have learned in the midst of my healing.

I am a part of every story I write. But this is the first time the story I wrote has been reflected back into my life in such a powerful way. The goodness in the green velvet has changed my life. I, too, have tried on the green velvet dress that we used for the play. And to my utter joy it fit me! I am one of the women who has been touched by its goodness, beauty, and truth.

My prayer and hope are that you will be, too.

This is a place for you to write your embroidered life legacy in a sentence or two.
Think about Emma, Rachel, Laurel, and Julie when you scribe yours.
Don't forget to sign it and date it.

❧ ACKNOWLEDGEMENTS ❧

Nothing of worth and value is ever created without the help of incredible people. Here are some of mine:

Gary Bayer, mentor of my writing and storytelling for more than 30 years; home with Jesus 2017. *Marla Yoell* for whom the character 'Marla Bradshaw' is named; home with Jesus 2018. *Linda Rand,* you have a theater now — Rand Theater; home with Jesus 2019.

David, Gracie, and *Tim,* for the incredible love and family support I have received each day.

Annie Baldwin, my incredible Book Assistant, or as she prefers to be called "Your Majesty of Process and Publication." Your joy brought joy to all of it!

Marcia Coppess, my only ever incredible editor. She's the best there is. She hears my storyteller and always brings out the better story in me.

Vicki and *Val,* the beloved and dear midwives of *The Green Velvet Christmas Dress.*

Janelle Kujath, the book's sweet and compassionate Illustrator. She paints from the heart!

Joshua Petrillo, the cover's design and book's graphic artist, formatting and paginating all things that make our book look like a real book. And he's just an all-around great person, too!

Kathy Wood, the quiltmaker and designer of Marla's quilt as suggested by the book.

Trenton Waterson, a true champion of story, film and the heart of all artists.

Ayanna Heidelberg, photography, advertising help, and humor.

Pastor Jack and Valarie Hayford; Dennis and Melinda Jernigan and *Annē J. Kay; Robbie Crawford, and Varetta Heidelberg* — support and kind words.

Perry Moore dearest brother, friend, and comrade in creativity.

Christy Cameron for embodying Emma and her likeness on the book cover.

Yuko and Jim real people from a journey in a hospital.

The Keepers Of The Green by way of support and prayer: My sisters Melanee N. & Margie and Larry B., Neilson Family, Juliana N., Deborah B., Vicky and Jim E., Renee' H., Varetta H., Ayanna H., Susie W., Margie R., Julie K., Margie C., Joyce V., Bea G., Kathy and Allen W., Holly B., Cindy B., Kathy H., Terri C., Allison and David M., Tegra and Marc L., Sarah G., Chloe G., Marianne C., Maureen and Lance B., Pedro and Ronnie N., Charisse and Wallace B., Olga W., Cari and Michael B-T., Jen and Ryan S., Lindi K., Myers Family, Linda and Shirley R., Sharon and Bob D., Ayline T., Perry and Jen M., Susan and Kevin F., David Buller, Sandy B. and her mom, Cathy D., Lynn C., Nancy R., Melissa K., Tina O., Christy and Dave C., Sherrell and Adam A., Pastor Ken and Lori Andrews, Pastor Ron and Stephanie Bloom, Pastor James and Kelly North, Theresa and Phil C., Robin and Kelly R., Gene and Deedie S., Prudence and Shaleah D., Debbie and Al N., Jeanne W., Gloria and Dale B., Baker and Yoell families, my Montrose Church's women's Bible study small group, The Barn Bible Study Gals of Caruthers, CA, my home church of Fellowship Church, Pasadena

"The Ladies of The Velvet," the sweet saints and pastors of First Presbyterian Church, Newhall.

Those who contributed to the production costs for this book. I thank you for your generosity!

And most of all to the Father, Son and Holy Spirit — the mysterious three in one — that always long to write the better Story in all of us, with gratitude to the Author and Finisher of my faith. Hallelujah!

⬧ FOR YOUR INFORMATION ⬧

Dennis Jernigan
Shepherd's Heart Music
Dennisjernigan.com
Allinallchurch.com

Melinda Jernigan
Mpdesignsjewelry.com

Varetta Heidelberg
VarettaHeidelberg.com

Perry Moore
reverbnation.com/perrymoore

The Barn Bible Study Gals of Caruthers, CA
RobbieM.Crawford@hotmail.com

Joshua Petrillo
facebook.com/wonderboxdesign

GriefShare
griefshare.org

ABOUT THE AUTHOR: MELEA J. BROCK

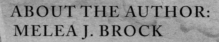

For more than 30 years Melea J. Brock has been writing and telling stories *for the child inside all of us* under the banner of Right-Side-Up Stories for Upside-Down People. She has written and produced numerous books, audios, and plays, and has been featured in magazines as well. *The Green Velvet Christmas Dress* is by far her largest adventure in publishing. A play is one thing, a collection of short stories another, but this novella seemed huge in comparison. The play's success spurred Melea to write the book, adding more identifiable male and female characters and many details that a play can't quite offer in its confined story telling. Melea's hope has always been to have her readers *step inside a story,* and to tell it out loud to others. "There is something wonderful that happens when we read to one another. First, relationship happens and second, we find our own personal stories interacting with the content, and within community. That's just fun, unpredictable, and highly memorable. Anything can happen in those short moments of the telling of a story together… anything."

Melea makes her home in Southern California with her husband, David, and their grown adult-sized amazing children.

More information, products and copies of *The Green Velvet Christmas Dress* can be located at rightsideupstories.com. Contact Melea directly with comments or questions at mjbstory@gmail.com.

ABOUT THE ILLUSTRATOR: JANELLE KUJATH

Janelle Kujath is an artist who is currently based in Colorado. She began painting and drawing in 1999, and is largely self-taught in illustration and painting. She is known for her work in acrylic and oil-based portraits and landscape illustrations. Trained in psychology, Janelle often shapes her work to speak to an individual and meet them where they are in life. When Melea approached her to be the illustrator of *The Green Velvet Christmas Dress*, Janelle began by drawing and sketching each scene of the story, but soon came to realize there was something missing. The illustrations were lacking the depth and emotions that each scene deserved, and she felt these elements would be best communicated through her palette of acrylic paint. The images throughout the book are individual paintings completed on their own separate canvas. Janelle resides in Parker, Colorado with her husband, loving golden retriever, and new baby girl.

Contact Janelle at janellekujath@gmail.com

THIS EDITION IS A LIMITED NUMBERED & SIGNED COPY

Number _____ of _____

Hope